Additional Praise for
The Great American Suction

"In David Nutt's luminous debut novel, the perennially put-upon protagonist's existence consists of a daisy chain of half-baked calamities. A brain-damaged post-postmodern anti-hero, Shaker's a not-so-innocent Josef K. for the culture that births precocious meth chefs and celebrity impersonator wannabes. Dystopian, and by that, I mean contemporary, this debut ratchets up the possibilities of prose with its stylistic virtuosity while laying bare the toxic underbelly of the garbage art crowd. If you're a fan of David Ohle's *Motorman* or Sam Lipsyte's *Venus Drive*, *The Great American Suction* awaits you."

– Christopher Kennedy,
   author of *Clues from the Animal Kingdom*
   and *Ennui Prophet*

Tyrant Books

Via Piagge Marine 23
Sezze (LT) 04018
Italy

www.NYTyrant.com

ISBN: 978-0-9992186-3-1

First Edition

Book design by Adam Robinson
Cover design by Brent Bates

The Great American Suction

David Nutt

*For loved ones lost and living,
strangers, enablers, foes, and friends.*

But mostly, mostly for Gina.

PART ONE

1.

Morning has broken on Shaker's pale sliver of
the republic. He holds himself upright on the riding
mower, his feet slotted in stirrups, racing the machine in
wide swaths around the yard. His hair is blasted up, and
his face feels rubbery in the hard wind. And the noise.
All this machinery roaring into him. The rest of the yard
crew is sculpting the topiary at a leisurely pace. The
houses in this neighborhood are not upscale, but neither
are they slums. Their windows are full of people—slurry
shapes of them, whole congregations—watching Shaker
and his cohort beautify their property for an insufficient
wage. After completing each circuit, Shaker salutes the
windows, but nobody ever salutes back. He's wearing
rounded, black sunglasses and a seasonal tan. When
late autumn arrives and the grass stalls and the foliage
is raked up and bagged and deported, Shaker will be
unemployed until springtime. He's in hoarding mode
now. It makes him strangely reckless. Shaker is saluting
every man, oak, pillar, and shrub on site.

The cohort takes their lunch on the driveway's sunbaked blacktop, standing against the company truck like
homeless men in a police lineup. Shaker's ears are ringing so loudly he can't understand his coworkers' conversation. He hears only mumbles and thrum but nods
politely along. Finishing his tuna fish early, he kicks into

the stirrups and waits there, patient, stationary in his machine, an orange pair of gun-range earmuffs clamped on his head, which continues nodding, still nodding, always nodding.

*

The Yarn Barn is not such a nuisance to Shaker. His only protest is there isn't much barn in its appearance. And yet, Darb stands in front of the strip mall on his court-designated, three-foot-wide allotment of pitted sidewalk, the signboard leaned on his hip. Shaker has to tip his head sideways and squint to read this one. *Unravel the Yarn Barn Conspiracy* is inscribed in purple sharpie and shoe polish. Darb's knotty fingers and the groin of his jumpsuit are likewise blotched. Shaker itches his own chin stubble. He tries to nod intelligently. His cousin nods back at him while sipping something cranberry-colored from a crumple of Styrofoam. The sidewalk area around him is inundated, all variety of litter.

"It's a reverse drive-thru," Darb says. "They throw it at me, I abide. Just this morning, I got half a muffin sandwich, three French fry, and a melted Bomb Pop. They think they're being uncivil, but I'm flattered. Dumb shits."

Shaker swivels his head, but there is no one else on the premises. Only his cousin, teasing out a long tangle of ear fuzz, adding, "Our kind is not to be trifled with."

Shaker nods at this, stretching a leg that knocks over Darb's sign.

"Don't do that."

"I had a dream last night," Shaker says.

"How romantic."

"The dream was that I didn't recognize myself."

"No?" Darb asks, only half-listening.

"Like someone had glued another man's face atop my face. Kinda freaky."

Shaker shrugs and shuffles in place. He realizes he's still pawing his chin.

"Let's get uncorked," Shaker says.

"You treating?"

"I am not."

"My funds are slumped. All my shoe polish is gone."

"I see that."

Among the detritus at Darb's feet is a selection of empty cat food tins. Darb's mouth is stained a mild brown. He follows Shaker's gaze and grins. "Poppin' 'em open is like pulling a grenade pin. I use my teeth, heave 'em overhand after I'm sated."

"Sounds dubious," says Shaker.

"I got a whole coupon *book*."

"Can we get any beers with it?"

"It's feeling more like a whipped cream afternoon. Suck aerosol and murder some brain cells. Relive our younger days."

Shaker chews his cheek. "My pantry has been bare a long time."

"I ain't even *got* a pantry."

"Doris?" Shaker asks.

"Think I'm allowed back in?"

"Maybe if you keep on your belly and try not to upset the furniture."

"I can do that, all of that."

"Doris," Shaker repeats, verifying his contribution to the day's agenda.

Darb offers him the last of the cranberry and fetches his signage from the dirt. "My baby," he whispers, brushing the sign until it is clean.

The cousins carry themselves against the loud tide of traffic to Doris's meticulously maintained A-frame, which seems a direct reproach to the shoddiness her neighbors are cultivating in aluminum and junk. A long-time widow, Doris doesn't stray much from the house anymore. But she lets all sorts of stray men inside. Ten years of sordid rumor and the woman has relaxed into the gothic reputation. She is sitting on the parlor room futon in only a towel and hair rollers, her bangs pinned up from the cream on her face, tiny blooms of cotton swab partitioning her toes.

"Please and thank you," Darb says, entering without a knock. Shaker follows him into the fog of toenail varnish, ammonia odors. "We have come to be creamed and whipped."

"Batten the hatches and nail down the credenza," Doris replies.

"That's a hot look you're wearing."

"Some men could love it."

"Imagine," Darb grunts, down on his knees and pillaging the mini-fridge.

"Shaker," says Doris.

"Ma'am?"

"You are the gentleman your cousin will never allow himself to be trained to be."

"That makes him sound like a circus bear."

"What's so wrong with that?"

"Look at the steep recession of that hair. He can't be a bear if he's bald."

Doris rolls her eyes. "Is that what passes for wit on your end of the island?"

"What island?"

"Don't be a rube."

"Maybe I'm a rube," Shaker shrugs.

"My god, there isn't much wet gray stuff left between your ears, is there? Maybe that's what makes you such a gentleman."

"I'm not so gentle," Shaker mumbles.

"A torrid love affair might change that."

"She means fornication," Darb says, head in the fridge.

"Please don't be despicable, darling."

"I'm not easily romanced, either," says Shaker as he envisions his seduction: nude and unshaven on a motel bed, in the final throes of heart failure, a fit of stroke, while the maid staff gathers around the mattress debating how best to change the sheets.

"I guess not," Doris sighs. "You emanate that middling vibe no sane woman wants to mingle her chromosomes with."

Shaker nods.

"Stop nodding," she says. "I just insulted you."

"I've had it worse."

"Those seasonal employments of yours."

"Yards this month. I ride a giant machine."

"Dreadful."

"It keeps the dog in Purina."

"Shaker, you don't have a dog."

"No," he says. "I do not."

Voracious inhalation sounds are radiating from behind the open mini-fridge door, a portion of Darb's scraggy scalp. Doris unscrews a jar of avocado skin ointment and begins rubbing it into her bunions.

"The man who used to live across the way? He was another gentleman type, handsome, good build. Dumb as a poodle. One day, he left the house all spruced and spangled in a new suit and came home with a snub-nosed revolver, one of those little cutie-pie guns. You know the type?"

"I know the type."

"He sprayed his brain gore all over the bath. Landlord said the cleanup required two bottles of Lysol and six rolls of paper towels. The rest flushed right down. Imagine, Shaker. Half a century of handsome life on this lame, flying rock, and all it takes to wipe it up is twenty bucks' worth of custodial product."

Shaker resists the urge to nod. From his current vantage beside the window, Doris's A-frame seems to be levitating. Shaker glances down and his vertigo stirs. He turns away from the window, turns to Doris and her mess of cosmetics, then Darb half-hidden in the mini-fridge, and finally to the mirror fastened with thumbtacks between two framed lithographs of children. Shaker doesn't recognize the children. They are smudged and antique-looking and comfortably caramelized in an earlier, more patrician era. In the mirror, something seems to be wrong with Shaker's face.

"Eureka!" Darb announces, kicking shut the fridge and sauntering back to the futon, head tilted at the ceiling, a can of whipped cream balanced on his large frontal lobe.

"Circus bear," Shaker admits.

Doris grins and takes careful aim at Darb's head with her electric bang curler, unplugged. "They always waltz right into the crosshairs," she says.

*

The frozen potpie has sat uneaten on the TV dinner tray in his TV-free den for hours. Shaker still can't rally an appetite. He remains pickled from the afternoon fumigation. It has been years since his last suck or huff. Paints and polish, commercial glues, kerosene clumped

12

with baby formula. Shaker very publically put it all up a nostril or into a lung at some point, and as a result he still enjoys VIP status at most retail hardware outlets in town. The methodology was elegant in its idiocy: absorb every industrial substance in the warehouse until the folds and ruts of his wrinkly prune brain had been ironed flat. Pause. Retch. Repeat. Only on occasion would Shaker find himself in a modest coma on some stranger's rug—his mind purged, his pants at half-mast—attempting to piss a spectacular arc over the living room couch. That was the extent of his debauch. It seemed less a compromise of ideals than an exploration of what lay beneath those ideals in the first place.

Shaker is loafing tonight on the rear porch he shares with the other half of his duplex. The sun has turned a weak blood color, and it can barely hold Shaker's attention. A cold wind blows through the middle of his skull. Shaker imagines his tortured brain cells decamping from his head in deerskin canoes as he waves goodbye to the shrinking armada, the horizon so small it hurts. Dimming. He is dimming. Shaker wakes from the reverie and notices the Hooster girl is reclined in his foldable beach chair, her body bikini'd, some miniscule technology plugged into the sides of her head. Her eyes are cupped by ping-pong ball slices.

"They have moved the sun to China for the evening," he says. "Should be back sometime in April."

"You're hovering like a cretin."

"This porch is shared."

"I've heard that," the Hooster girl says.

"That's my beach chair your skinny bricks are sprawled in."

"It's Mama's chair. You sold it last winter."

"Leased," Shaker says. "There's a scrap of paper somewhere to that effect."

The girl lifts a ping-pong ball hemisphere and peers at Shaker, a suspicious skew in the look.

"China maybe," he adds.

"Have you heard the new one?" she asks.

"Specifics, please."

"The college station is playing it as a joke. They call it pop smear. Just dial-tone noise and drum machines. Certainly no 'Drinker's Elbow' or 'Do-Si-Do Polygamy,' but it's a real heart-squelcher, and she's still our only local legend."

"I won't listen to it."

"You *been* listening to it. We can hear the crackle and fuzz through the drywall."

"Oh."

"She was your *wife*."

Shaker flinches at the word.

"Buy yourself a newer radio," says the girl. "Lift some weights while you're at it. Bulk up. Girls love a vain girth. Bench-press something."

"I found your mother's Pilates mat hanging out of the trash last week. Seemed salvageable. Is there a video-tape that goes with it? A TV? It might be nice having a TV again. What exactly is a Pilates?"

"*Gawd*!!!" the girl near-shrieks.

Shaker can only shrug. "I suffered a blitz of the interior today. A kind of lapse."

"Specifics, please," she says in an adenoidal approximation of his voice that forces every muscle in Shaker's face to slacken. Layers and layers of mournful flab.

"Forget it."

"Everybody has a few laps in them," says the girl behind her ping-pong balls again. "Then they peter out to shit. It happens. Mostly to cretins."

"You have missed my point." Shaker knocks a bottle of tanning lotion with his foot, then stands several pensive minutes at the cusp of backyard, not admiring the stretch of bald dirt, not even looking at it. Just sort of tottering there.

2.

Saturday night has arrived, but Shaker can't
locate himself inside it. Instead, he feels stationed at
the far rim, peering in with bland expression, wanting
to hum but not. He is unmoored on these weekend
evenings when his yard employment is paused, his silent
apartment hollers at him, and the radio will only attract
classical rhapsodies that for certain philosophic reasons
Shaker cannot endorse. So once his freeze-dried dinner
is digested and his teeth have been almost homicidally
brushed, Shaker makes the short trudge to town. Main
Road is a two-and-a-half-block stretch of pawnshop
splendor anchored by a fried-chicken franchise that only
operates between the hours of midnight and four, when
the bars have released their stink-breathed denizens into
the night and nobody can find the correct car to unlock.
It's a vivid scene: dozens of drunks leaned against their
vehicles, jamming their keys in wrong holes with great
experiment. But it's not that hour yet. The bars are still
brimming, and Shaker enters the Regal Beagle. Only
a few heads in here, token slumps of shoulder, a man
prying his buck knife from the dartboard cork. Shaker
bobs his head to the crenulated punk noise the juke is
blaring. He takes a stool. The bartender, Tobin, holds
a semi-clean glass under the establishment's only
functioning tap while Shaker does the stoic nod thing.

He accepts the pint with a grunt and drains it in one or two parched gulps. Shaker feels good. He feels hoisted. He digs up his money for another round and finds his wallet is parched as well.

"Shitsky," Shaker says.

"You okay, Shaker?"

Shaker considers the question for a tense minute and quietly replies, "They're putting the continents back together with scotch tape."

Tobin leans over the bar and examines the bare fold of fake leather in Shaker's hands. "That is an enormous shame."

"Only a couple bucks. I'm good for it."

"The most you are good for, Shaker, is making the case for stricter birth control."

Shaker gives Tobin a pleading look.

"No pleading," Tobin says.

"But I'm a buddy."

"I'm all booked up on buddies tonight. I'd rather redecorate my home with the staved-in skulls of dead-beats, assorted freeloaders, and other once-beautiful children." Tobin leans towards Shaker and inquires, "What size are you around the neck?"

Shaker tries to smile, but Tobin has already whistled for Howie "The Howitzer" Pulasko, a muscle-bloated bouncer overdone in salmon polo and unnaturally pleated khaki shorts that reveal too much tendon in the thigh. Shaker admires the sartorial boldness, but his own innards—all eighteen spools of them—are in recoil mode. The Howitzer has an arm around Shaker, who has an arm around his guts, trying to bucket them.

"Shaker here thinks the Beagle has turned non-profit," says Tobin.

Shaker nods and feels the arm around him, the room, the weight.

"It's a noble cause," he says.

"I'd pitch in a ten spot," somebody grumbles, "to watch Howie dismantle him like one of them artificial Christmas trees."

The heads have gathered, and various voices agree. Scandalously, so does Shaker. "But I'd have to borrow the ten spot," he shrugs.

"Shaker?"

"Ignore me."

"Pinky or thumb?" Tobin asks.

The Howitzer holds Shaker's wrist in a puddle of beer suds as Tobin produces a mallet tethered to the cash register with nylon rope. He holds it overhead, a Nordic warrior pose, and hums a medieval dirge. There's simply too much pinky in the world, thinks Shaker, unable to shut his eyes against the spectacle. The heads are hushed. Then Tobin sets aside the mallet and smacks Shaker a hard one on the cheek.

"Your punishment, deadbeat, is to hustle over to my house barefoot and give my beagle dog his heartworm medication."

"I am sans auto," says Shaker.

"Better get started then," Tobin tells him. "I'm over on Spruce."

"That's six miles."

"Six and a half."

"Barefoot?"

"It's the only brown house. Door's unlocked. Pills are in the cabinet. Mena is doing her go-go gig tonight so it's just Prince-Prince at home."

"The beagle," says Shaker.

"Bare feet are optional."

Shaker leans out of the Howitzer's hug and glares at the window. "Looks like flurries."

"It's August out there, Shaker."

"Sledding," he whispers.

Two steps on the sidewalk and already the wind is rubbing the feeling off his face. August, yes, but unruly. These crazed breezes invade at night, knocking around traffic signals and turning TV aerials into lethal javelins that can be found stabbed among rows of pretzeled patio equipment the next morning. Shaker has to hopscotch through a slick spread of bakery trash. There are loaves in pile, muffin crusts, aborted dough. He pockets a chocolate éclair to pacify the mongrel mutts in his neighborhood, assuming he ever returns home, and he continues down the road's middle, thumb up, half-hoping to flag a ride. He has already mulled his various escape routes and excuses and alibis, but he feels somehow committed to the mission. Make the trek. Go to dog. Save dog. Try not to draw homeward any more hungry strays. He imagines this endangered breed of beagle flopped on the kitchen tile, neglected and nursing a calamitously wormed heart. Then he pictures a funeral service for the animal, a stone memorial in a public park somewhere, Shaker weeping on the sidelines. The distance is only six miles, six and a half. Shaker forces each leg forward and tries to remember the last time he heard any rumor about wayward hitchhikers blown off the tarmac by mysterious winds.

Mainly, he misses his old auto. A two-tone, white-and-red-paneled utility van in which Shaker installed a plywood loft for the storage and transportation of musical equipment, back in the days he roadied on the local bar band scene. That was how he met his future ex-wife, the National Sensation. She was fronting her first band at the time, The Fake American Embolism, a scrum of heartsick thugs, blue-skinned alcoholics, and moonlighting attorneys who specialized in twangy heartland rock. Shaker watched them perform in every rural tavern and spaghetti restaurant across Ohio, one godless sandbox after another, Shaker always occupying the middle of the floor, rocking his head at radically unmusical tempos and suppressing a lustful moan, while the young woman cavorted in her own private funnel of spotlight onstage.

His nickname for her was either a snarky flirt or flirty snark; Shaker was never sure which. Soon enough he and the National Sensation slept together, cohabitated, broke up, slept together again, eloped. He helped her christen the next incarnation of her band—The Proud American Stigmata—and she promoted Shaker from occasional roadie to touring bassist, although he had never touched a guitar in his life. He was confounded by the length and ballast of the instrument. Playing it was like bearing down on a span of suspension cable with only a Q-tip. Also, he never really mastered the art of plugging the thing in. His new wife's musical tastes were already mutating from country-western to more adventurous genres—experimental punk, avant trash rock, urban noise—that were not sought much on the county fair circuit. The band was demoted from outdoor amphitheaters to VFW halls and basement squats, smaller and smaller rooms. Shaker found himself likewise demoted after his wife met a millionaire venture capitalist whose idea of a relaxing evening cocktail was double-malt scotch mixed with sheep placenta and human blood. Shaker's six-month marriage was dissolved with a sticky note she left affixed to the fridge: *My dearest glue-sniffing spouse. Don't forget to sweat the eggplant. Gone forever, N.S.* Shaker lurched around the motel kitchenette, squinting at the kinks and ligaments of her eloquent cursive through a muddle of tears. His own fingertips twitching, he knew, on all the wrong notes.

Now his ex-wife haunts him across a global cartel of corporatized media—print, radio, TV.

And Shaker faints at the merest whiff of eggplant.

*

Spruce Road is a backwater artery without commercial or industrial properties that lacks the civic infrastructure granted most third-world hamlets. The streets aren't lit or paved, the homes are not reservoir fed. The region is policed solely by local militia, which itself is only a two-man operation. The Brothers Tully. The fraternal pair were long ago banished from the National Guard for mutinous conduct and have since parlayed their military training into a career of community harassment and black marketeering. Unfortunately, the Tullys are not present to help Shaker establish which of these brown homes belongs to Tobin. There are five. Shaker tiptoes around the isolated properties, hunched low and feeling like a skeezy pervert. He removes his black windbreaker and prays the white undershirt will broadcast his innocence as an honest amigo par excellence. He's willing to be shot dead for a cause, just not an ironic one.

Then Shaker sights a weight-bench in a side yard and decides he has found the correct home. He bangs the mud from his boots, scales the porch, but the door is locked. Definitely brown, he thinks, surveying the shanty from each angle. Shaker putters a bit. The windows are shut, the blinds drawn, a soft sepia glows behind the panes. Shaker arranges himself into a skeptical comport and realizes: Tobin is testing him. Will Shaker tromp all this way only to slink back to the bar in wretched defeat? Will he stand around like a skeezy perv and gaze at the locked shanty until Tobin or his stripper girlfriend meanders up the driveway in a few hours' time? Will Shaker heft a rock and shatter a window, mindless of consequence and without clobbering the dog?

About the dog: Shaker hasn't heard any barks or rampant licking or canine snores. Maybe the heartworm has hollowed the poor animal already. Make your mistake, Shaker thinks. Just make it quickly. And so he gets a running start and rams the door and feels everything— wood, bone, lacquer, world—give way at once. Shaker bursts through with such momentum he slams into an immediate wall, whirls, folds, and is rug-sprawled a solid minute or so, idly inspecting his freshly sprained collarbone, until he glances around and notices the Brothers Tully reclined in identical BarcaLoungers, a wall of mounted antlers and shotguns framing them in redneck tableau.

"What have you done with the dog?" Shaker asks, realizing there is no dog. Only the older Tully Brother reaching lazily for a long-barreled elephant gun. The other Brother is trying to peer around Shaker to the widescreen TV. Shaker can't resist. He follows the militiaman's sightline and sees the image on screen. Shaker's ex-wife is romping around a historic pavilion with a Union Jack flag shawled around her shoulders, shrieking into an air traffic controller headset as she dismembers a mannequin replica of Betsy Ross with a smoky chainsaw. Behind her, a spangled backdrop announces *The Fake American Orgasm*. The program is some sort of tabloid hagiography, the kind of gossipy entertainment show that Shaker used to watch with the sound muted and his nasal cavity reamed with aerosol propellant or VCR head cleaner. This particular episode includes a rapid-fire montage of potato-faced pundits sweating profusely under studio makeup and blathering about this renegade musician's chameleon aesthetics, bootstrap ethos, cutthroat biz sense. *Her authenticity.* One of the TV commentators refers to Shaker's ex, without acid or sarcasm, as an unparalleled purveyor of the American Absurd. A chorus of smarm agrees.

Shaker lifts a leg and turns off the TV with his big toe. Realizing, also, one of his boots has been flung wide and rests among pebbles and shells at the bottom of a burbling fish tank. The TV button, Shaker notes with no small pleasure, feels rather warm on the toe.

"Seems I am the victim of the cosmic joke," Shaker says. "But the thing is? The joke? It's actually sorta *funny.*"

"Gentlemen," he adds, "my boot is poisoning your lichen."

Shaker returns his head to its comfortable cradle on the ground, staring at the creamily spackled ceiling. He's settling in for the imminent interrogation, the long torture, the longer shame. A gun barrel nudges him in the snout. Big toe still on the TV, Shaker clicks over to channel four, wheedles the volume control, and waits for the next round of entertainment—an international rugby match in which each team is foundering badly at the wrong end of the field—to resume.

3.

Shaker's furniture has started to slowly creep
away from him. His share of the duplex is already a
spartan kind of deal. The change is blatant enough. So
he marks his folded metal chairs and card table and the
one grimy throw rug with chalk, noting their new angles
and positions, their late-hour shadows steep in the sun.
The next day, the furniture and chalk silhouettes have
migrated a few subtle inches eastward. It's almost as
if the whole living room lifted up on one leg and all its
contents slid loose. Shaker heads outside and asks the
Hooster girl if he slept through an earthquake.

"You on drugs?" she replies.

"Not anymore."

"Maybe it's time you start again," she says.

*

Doris rides in the backseat behind a barricade of the
only carpentry materials Shaker owns: hammer, rake,
garden hose, four nails pried from the Hooster half of
the porch, and a plastic sick bucket that Doris is trying to
hold away from her face. She is chaperoning today's field
trip because she does not trust her Skylark in Shaker's
custody. "Also," she explained while watching Shaker
white-knuckle his way out of her driveway, "I suppose
everyone needs a small catastrophic adventure now and
again to remember why they haven't been leaving the

barracks." Shaker is still thinking this over. He sits up front, settled snugly into the blistered vinyl, steering with one hand, a supply of timber buckled beside him. The sun ignites the car's chrome trim like gold foil. It seems to Shaker he has suddenly found conveyance vis-à-vis the world's most expensive condom wrapper.

"We *are* the maniacs," Shaker says agreeably.

*

He is three days into the repair, but he still swings with too much shoulder, still misses nails, hammers thumb and forefinger, struggles to keep his materials steady. He is braced with an elbow against the doorframe, the sun warm on his neck, while the Brothers Tully watch from their ugly crease of lawn. Both men wear the seriousness and deliberation of spelling bee judges. Shaker hits the frame and slants it. He straightens it and starts again.

"Anyone got a bevel square? A tape measure? Rope and crane?"

Shaker looks over his shoulder. The Tullys are into another six-pack, their empties screwed neck-first into the dirt. Doris remains in the car with a celebrity tabloid that contains a two-page full-color spread on Shaker's ex-wife and her latest bistro rampage. Shaker has an extra nail between his teeth. He spits the nail into his palm and hacks up something unpleasant and orange from inside his lungs. His middle moves, an uneasy tide. Kicking at the frame, he tells the Tullys, "A little glue, a little paint. *A lot* of paint."

Brother Two underarms a beer at Shaker, and Shaker catches the bottle in his shirt, startled by his own whiplash reflex. "Maybe tomorrow," he says.

The Brothers grumble.

"Tuesday?"

Twin nods.

"Tuesday." Shaker takes an interminable sip and drains the bottle. He puts the bottle in his bucket, along with his handkerchief and nails and imitation Ray-Bans, and he carts his supplies to the car, where Doris is already retreating to the backseat. Her tabloid on the dashboard displays a paparazzi snapshot of Shaker's ex-wife in incognito tracksuit and black mod wig, hiding her sunglassed face behind carryout coffee as she kicks a pedestrian in the crotch. At least he thinks it's his wife. Her Ray-Bans look to be the real item. Shaker swats the magazine to the floor, then picks it up and neatly rubs it shut.

Doris has the radio cranked, a testosterone-rich stadium anthem, but Shaker turns the noise off. The Skylark is stopped at a traffic signal, and there is movement in the dirty panes. A parade of children. They are marching homeward from some type of parochial education, uniformed in gray argyle and strapped into their backpacks like tiny paratroopers, toting lunchboxes and bruised apples and broken sticks. Each child takes a turn leering into the sedan with a manic expression. Shaker wants to pull some ghoulish faces of his own, contort his cheeks, expand his nostrils, wag tongue and wave hello, but he cannot. He simply cannot.

*

Tonight, the Hooster woman and girl are filling their territory with insistent bicker. Shaker understands the general tenor of the argument, but the petty details elude him. Competing strains of dancehall music shiver up the walls. The woman and girl bark in the same brittle register, their voices acquiring strange regional accents the louder they go. They bang their silverware and take turns slamming the toilet seat. They drag their garbage bins too late to the curb and leave them abused by the elements all week. Shaker knows there is an awkward progenitor situation. He knows these arguments reduce to smaller and smaller themes. Like Shaker, their household is held hostage on a daily basis by the bloodless whims of the banal. Do the woman and girl also shun rayon? Do they believe the skin cream commercials? Should it be a turnpike world or a trolley world? Margarine or the other stuff? Some evenings—after a long day of dwindling portions—the banal buttresses them all quite nicely.

Standing in his entranceway, Shaker is marinating in these and other small mysteries when his eyes focus upon the imposing scale of the Howitzer filling Shaker's kitchen. The man's broad back is turned. The water is running. The Howitzer is washing Shaker's dirty flatware in Shaker's dirty sink.

"Almost done here," the bouncer says.

Shaker is too stunned to shut the door. He dodders on one foot, then the other, feeling disproportioned, kind of brain-heavy.

"You're letting in a draft," the Howitzer tells him and indicates the luminous dishware on the countertop. "You should really get yourself a drying rack, Shaker."

Shaker may be rundown with worry and maybe a foreign germ or two, but the vision seems genuine. The Howitzer resumes rinsing a selection of chintzy plastic knives included in a pumpkin-carving kit. Shaker once assembled the kits for cash. He kept one, just one for himself, and has endured a nagging guilt ever since. He wonders if the Howitzer's tetanus shots are up to date. He notices, not without a mild voltage of terror, the Howitzer is wearing rubber gloves. Shaker owns none.

"How's Tobin's dog?" Shaker asks. "Its heartworms. Its *heart*."

"Oh, you don't need to worry about that."

"Well," Shaker says. "What do I need to worry about?"

"Don't forget that drying rack," the Howitzer replies, cranking off the faucet's flow and moving around Shaker to exit the still gaping door, he and his gloves, gone. Shaker is left to stare slackly around his kitchen, noticing now the rust barnacles are chiseled off the toaster, the sink is spotless, the pantry dusted, the scrub brush replenished with a superior brand of detergent.

His whole house has been cleaned.

4.

Shaker is reclined on the beach chair with his radio in his lap, slumbering to a soundtrack of rock-hipster laments, the preening clang of prefab angst and fashionable haircuts. He roared around on his machine for most of the morning, massacring the yards of accountants and morticians and other esteemed members of the professional caste, and he knocked a corner off a hedgerow that he tried to piece back together with wire and post until his supervisor put him on peony detail for the rest of the day. Now his attempt at beach chair sloth is interrupted by some occult force. Shaker wakes in a rush, clung with sweaty cotton. He has missed the sunset completely, and somebody has removed the batteries from his radio. The Hooster girl. She has a hula-hoop around her arm and wears a nasty glare.

"Mama says she heard shrieking."

"Out here?"

"You look like you just climbed out a sauna."

"Several," Shaker mumbles, unbuttoning his top and penultimate buttons, airing his burgeoning heatstroke.

"You're taking up all the good patio, too."

Shaker looks around, grabs a broom, and uses it to oar-row himself and the chair backwards a few feet. "Nice hula-hoop."

"Don't be a skeezy perv."

"What?"

"*Perv*," she says.

"I feel snowed in," Shaker shrugs. "That's all."

The Hooster girl's face is red as rare steak, her freckles lost in the swell of blush. She hands him the hoop and stands at the far end of the porch with her arms pressed in, a slim rod of girl ready for the horseshoe. "Ring me," she says.

Shaker misses by a leg. His second throw is even worse. Then he hoops her on the third try.

"Frisbee is my one true calling," he says.

"About your wife—"

"Wife? I have no wife."

"Mama says you're a lonely man who's sitting around waiting for some honest amigo to come pull the plug." The girl arranges her arms on her chest, shifts to one leg, a flamingo stance. "Mama's new guy socked her so hard in the face she can't wear sunglasses."

"Sorry to hear that."

"Mama's plug gets pulled every damn day."

"I don't know the secret."

"Yeah," the girl says. "No shit."

"Tell me the next time he comes around. The face socker."

"Like you'd do anything from that lazy chair."

Shaker shrugs.

"You already had one visitor tonight," she tells him.

"I did?"

"The crazy sign guy."

"My cousin."

"Everyone hates that guy."

"I've heard that."

"He was banging on your front door, trying to jimmy your windows. Mama had to chase him off with a shish-kebab skewer. That dude looked *rough.*"

"I like shish kebabs," Shaker replies.

"He looked just as bad as you."

Shaker waits for the girl to depart, and then he rears back his head, sucks some deep-rooted phlegm from the recesses of his throat, and launches it skyward, aiming for the fleeing sunlight and missing it by just this much.

*

The wheeled cart is loaded with black bags, tube apparatus, a pungent cargo. The cart's operator is one of Shaker's yard crew, a pill-and-pipe addict who also has a special fondness for chinchillas and mixed martial arts, named Thin. He's waiting outside the town head shop with one hand hooked on his belt loop, the other shakily harvesting snot crust from his nostril. He wears the sloughed-off expression of a meatloaf drooping under too many watts. Inside the shop, Shaker recognizes the tortured profile of Thin's roommate, the Minnesotan, bent over a case of bongworks and pipes. The Minnesotan is shellacking the glass with his saliva, several lustrous coats. Back on the sidewalk, Thin is ready to wheel onward until Shaker blocks the path of his cart. "Almost didn't recognize you without the Weed Eater strapped around your waist."

"Yeah, that's me," replies Thin. "Mr. Weed Eater. That's me full time."

Each of Thin's nostrils gives a rabid twitch, like a rodent deranged on pharmaceuticals. One of his precious chinchillas, perhaps. A month ago, Shaker saw the man rove his Weed Eater over his own sneaker, ventilating the toe tip. And the expression on Thin's face when it happened, a *bored* expression, unimpressed.

Thin impatiently jiggles his overloaded cart, a silver cage on three wheels.

"Missing a wheel," Shaker says.

"Only supposed to have three."

"Looks tipsy."

"You're blocking my way, hoss."

"Just a sidewalk," Shaker says.

Thin tames his nostrils, looks up into the lamplight without blinking or flaring anything, and looks back at Shaker, the same lidless stare.

"Hear you taken up with Tullys," he says.

The corners of Shaker's mouth are dry, too dry. "I owe them some work."

"That right?"

"Just a day or two more."

"Got a question for you, Quaker."

"It's Shaker."

"Why you think there ain't any jobs for us after November?"

Shaker shrugs. "Nothing to rake or mow," he says.

"Can you salt, shovel, plow?"

"Sure," Shaker slow-nods.

"It's a whole skill set," smiles Thin. "And there's a lot of fat contracts with the township to do winter work. Roads, parking lots, libraries, facilities. You got any idea why we're not doing it?"

"Nada."

"Those militia twins got connections, back-channel, black-market, under-table shit. It's all monopolized, man! Fucking Tullys run the show! And you're in bed with the enemy. You're in the muck."

Shaker tries to smile, but it feels like his face is yawning apart at the seams. Thin jiggles the cart back onto its three wheels and sneers, "Dude, you don't even mow that machine *straight.*"

Later that night, Shaker sits for some soup in Crimon's Diner, where he slurps his creamy tomato goulash in relative calm, wondering if maybe the Tullys might use their institutional strings to sling him better work. They have transportation at least, affiliations, repute. Meanwhile, the lawns are beginning to go dormant and the muck is encroaching. Shaker could use a brief sabbatical from the muck. He shifts his attention to a TV held by brackets above the hostess station and the familiar image on screen. His ex-wife, the National Sensation. The TV shows her flanked by a coven of bald and cragged attorneys in some stark courtroom scene, an ocean of faceless spectators smeared with the background, unfinished. It's a sketch artist's rendering. Shaker is sure it is her. The shapeless muumuu sack dress under a bouffant wig. Her pouty lips fixed in a mercenary smirk. Shaker lets the word *mercenary* soften in his mouth like a piece of moldering fruit. He thinks he can hear whatever faltering hydraulics are located deep at the bowels of the earth, lugubrious and rain-gray, slowing to a sad, dry creak.

He doesn't bother deciphering the info ticker scrolling the bottom of the screen. The bad painting is enough. Shaker stands, shoves napkin and silverware in pocket, and slips noiselessly out the door, leaving his soup unfinished and the bill unpaid.

*

His cousin's apartment is a basement bunker with a single stone entrance. Shaker has arrived after midnight. No one answers, so he tries the landlord's apartment upstairs. The older man who opens the door is shirtless and saddled with nipples the size of sand dollars,

33

a copious girth. Shaker is made self-conscious about his own skinny holdings. Malnourished and rangy, he widens his mouth but cannot fit the "ummm, yeah, errr" sounds out.

"I'm awake anyway," the landlord says. "You look awful. Shit-colored. Dead. You suffer the insomnia, too?"

"Pretty much just coasting on thermals at this point."

"Want some warm milk? I boil it hot, so hot it scalds."

"Temperature hurts my teeth," says Shaker.

"Easy enough to fix that."

The man pops the upper shelf of denture from his mouth and rotates it in the porch light. Shaker's stomach performs a similar levitation and spin. "Please put those monsters back in."

The man shrugs and eats the fake ivories and grins, tight and crooked. He maintains a stance that gives too much view of all the fuzz he is amassing in his navel's tiny pucker.

"I'm here for my cousin," Shaker says.

"That wild goose is long gone."

"Gone where? He just stopped by my place last night."

"Wish I could help. Really do. Unfortunately, Section Eights are notoriously fudgy. That moron could be anywhere. But let me just say, if he thinks he's getting his security deposit back—"

"This isn't about that."

"Not yet, it's not."

"Can I snoop around?" Shaker asks. "See what he left behind?"

"I hope you like crazy crap," the landlord replies.

Standing in the claustrophobic concrete hovel that Darb rented the last few years—four walls full of samurai blades and ninja chucking stars, a broken toilet, no radio, no TV—Shaker understands why he's never been invited inside. There isn't even enough clearance for Darb to practice marching with his sign, which rests in the corner, hemmed by a milk crate bookcase and urinated mattress.

"He paid $500 for this cave," Shaker says.

"Paid it happily."

"You took advantage."

"No more than anyone else," the landlord says.

Shaker examines the bookcase. Photocopied pamphlets and survivalist manuals and fliers and other paranoiac ephemera. Around it are taped pictures of cats, cat calendars, cat toys and cat knickknacks, all gruesomely defaced. Shaker peeks into a shoebox by the bed. His cousin's medication. Anti-depressants. Anti-psychotics. Reds and blues and greens. A whole anguished rainbow.

"You want any of this, take it now," says the landlord. "I got a new Looney Tune moving in next week."

Shaker considers snagging some kind of keepsake, a nostalgic totem of his cousin, but it's all accidental kitsch, dementia mementos, crazy crap.

"Have yourself a pleasant bonfire, I guess," Shaker says. He is squeezing through the cramped confines towards the door when the landlord grabs him.

"I saw your old lady on the news." The fat man grins, his dentures steady and fixed, and then the grin wanes. "Boy, you just can't hold onto a single goddamn thing, good or bad, can you?"

Shaker purses his lips tightly.

"You scare people, you know," says the man.

"My thermals," Shaker responds, pushing for the exit, "are thinning out."

*

The Hooster girl is asleep on the porch under a burlap blanket, her head plugged into a fragile, white device so small Shaker can barely read the print on its encasement. He lifts the iThing off the girl's stomach and inspects. He thumbs some buttons, but it won't scroll. A familiar refrain, tinny and digitized, crackles through the earpiece. The title track from the second LP, *The Unquiet American Coquetry Presents: Everything and Dander*.

She opens her eyes and looks up at Shaker holding her expensive toy, but she doesn't reach for it yet.

"You like this one," she says. "I always hear you turning it up."

"That's not me."

"This was your album. That's you on the bass, your sloppy filigree. You must have made money."

"Buried it all in the backyard. Right next to the dog."

"This song," she says. "I sorta hate it, and I sorta love it."

Shaker half-smiles.

"Years ago," he says, "my cousin had a habit of breaking into people's vehicles. Not to steal the car or soil it or anything. He just wanted to listen to the radio. He'd hotwire the thing and sit there, just listening to music until he fell asleep. People were always returning with their kids or their groceries to find their car door busted apart, the sound system cranked, this strange man snoring in the front seat with an iron file clenched in his fist like a conductor's baton. A real aficionado."

"I'd shoot him," the girl says.

"Repeatedly," Shaker nods.

She unplugs an earpiece and offers it up, but instead Shaker hands her the whole device.

"I didn't really play. Just held the thing. Mimed to a backing track. You know what the trick is on stage? Look bored. Everyone thinks you've been lifted into some higher rapture."

"People used to call you Shaker the Faker."

"I can't do the Charleston, either."

"That why she shot you in the chest?"

"Everyone adores that story," he says.

"Because it's a good story."

Shaker cracks a knuckle on the ledge of his chin and strains for a smile. He gets only a desultory lip twitch.

The Hooster girl sits up and drops her voice to a conspiratorial octave. "I bet she comes back here. Her and that rich husband she's got. After the lawsuits and court trials and bribes and settlements. I bet they snatch up all the land, all the fast-food joints and beautiful houses and idiot face-socking boyfriends. They buy it all and burn it all to the damn ground like it deserves to be damn burned."

"Except the yarn store. The yarn."

"Shaker," the girl says.

"It calms me," he shrugs.

The girl wraps the device in its earpiece cord and goes indoors, trailing her burlap to bed. Shaker nods goodnight and also retires, first to the kitchen and his trove of secret vodka, and then to the bathroom, where he stands five minutes outside the door, waiting patiently while whoever is inside finishes snaking the sink drain.

5.

Shaker's coworkers Thin and Munk and
Roderick Bartholomew are on their knees and hunched
forward so their bald craniums bulge in the sunlight as
they weed the overstuffed gutters. Their attention keeps
getting diverted by Shaker whorling around the property
at unsafe speeds, attempting to outrun their hard glares.
He has forgotten to wear his gun-range earmuffs today,
and the mower noise is creating dubious euphonies in
his head that Shaker tries to outrun, too. He downshifts
the machine and accidentally stalls. The warm fumes
updraft around him. His ears are ringing violently,
not just from engine noise but also the blood swishing
through his clenched ventricles, miles of pointless
tubing, heavy mortar in all his holes. Shaker is stranded
in the middle of the yard, some distance beyond himself.
For several hours, his supervisor—Hob Brock—has been
pruning a copse of weeping willows with what look to be
barbershop clippers. Hob rests his clippers and searches
Shaker for a sign. Shaker steps off the machine, circles
around, and stabs a finger skyward without looking.

"That seem like rain to anybody else?"

The sky is a pure, blissful, detergent-hued blue.
Shaker pretends not to notice Hob waving him over.
Instead, he turns and straps in, and with a debonair
flourish he restarts the machine.

*

After the unkempt grassland has been satisfactorily conquered, the men huddle in preparation for their weekend drug soiree. Shaker has been invited to similar soirees in the past but always declines because his life is not exactly lacking in blackouts, hangovers, bleak palls, and bleaker depressions. Amnesias, too. The men at their truck are also shunning him, although Shaker is angling for a ride home, so he moseys towards them with a sheepish look. Hob Brock stops him halfway.

"This ain't a rodeo, Shaker."

"I guess it's not," Shaker replies.

"You looked like a madman out there."

"Out there?" Shaker shades his forehead with his hand, poker visor-like, and surveys the neat, green yard. He can only see span, distance. Far-tapered edges. "I was expediting."

"You're gonna expedite yourself right out of a job."

"I'd hate to do that."

"Me too. You're the only clean beak here." Hob thumbs his nostril. Shaker can almost glean his point. "Even if that wasn't always the case."

Shaker is shucking his hard-rubber soles into the earth, embarrassed but also feeling a mite bit haughty. Then he turns his head and realizes the Weekend Party Truck has just rumbled off. Only Hob and Shaker remain. And then Hob leaves, too.

*

Darkness has settled in, and a spot lamp is rigged and aimed upwards, knocking Shaker's shadow against the house, a splayed and stretched double, so the real Shaker appears to be a marionette controlled by his larger, darker self. The Brothers Tully are lazing in the yard, watching Shaker try not to take off any more thumbnail

39

with that hammer. The door is intact and almost completely hung. Shaker has even added an extra sheet of paint, which did not dry properly before he began fitting the door on its replacement hinges. Maybe the wood has swollen, or the frame shrunk, or the paint was thicker than Shaker anticipated. He's randomly ramming away with his hammer, loud and wild and messily. But the door is no shabbier than the rest of the house. Shaker turns and shrugs.

"How long does it take the average person to hang and paint a door?" he asks them. "Six, seven months? That sound about right?"

Tully One looks at his double and hands him a fresh brew. Together, they sip and stare, sip and stare, drawing a steady bead on the sweat that has welled under Shaker's eyeballs, raw and stung with bloodshot.

"It's *winter* out here," Shaker says.

Idly, he juggles the hammer. The living room curtains are drawn back, and Shaker has a wide view of the furnishings and fixtures inside the Tully household. An array of taxidermy projects adorn the fireplace mantle. Squirrel, porcupine, turtle, raccoon. Shaker imagines a fishbowl that contains his own severed head, pale and macabre, wearing an expression of utmost leisure. He has no idea what he would say to it.

He also has no idea how long he spends leering into the Brothers' house. The spot lamp has been switched off, the Tullys gone inside. Shaker is standing alone with the Hooster girl's teal-painted bike leaned against a tree. The tree almost seems to sway as much as Shaker, his shadow, the larger world to which they may or may not still be bound.

*

The sun has yet to rise. Shaker goes barefoot to the kitchen and finds the faucet in the dark, guzzles from it clumsily, and—toweling his chin with his undershirt— he returns to the futon, where the Howitzer is taking a short rest. The man's speech has slowed, he's gesturing less vividly. These late-night invasions are siphoning some vital spunk from him. Shaker imagines a pace-maker seam across the Howitzer's sternum that once unzipped would reveal a vacuum-cleaner bag full with pruned organs and a metric ton of dry mulch. The vision consoles him somewhat. Then he slaps the man's shoul-der, and the Howitzer jerks awake.

"You must've been dreaming," says Shaker, pointing at the Howitzer's slurry chin puddle. "Got some residue on you."

"Doubtful," the Howitzer replies. "I have a pretty mundane inner life."

"Well, it leaks."

"And what about you, chief?"

"Me?"

"What is holding our good man Shaker together these days?"

"Bubblegum, hot solder, spiritual malaise. A whole lot of dried glue."

"How dry?"

"It's just glue," Shaker mumbles. "Old glue."

The Howitzer knuckles loose a sleep chigger from his eye socket. "Sometimes, when I turn off the lights at night, I see myself sitting at an enormous banquet table. I'm wearing a nice cloth seafood bib and hip sunglasses. The table is full of dead babies. Pieces, limbs, bones, all cooked in a pile. I've been ripping apart and eating them like fried chicken. Horrible, just horrible shit."

"But that's not a dream?"

"Maybe it's penance for some horribleness I've done in an earlier life. Or maybe a life that has yet to come. Maybe it's all the same thing."

"You believe that karma stuff."

"I think it's important for people like you to believe it."

"I see just fine up here in the nosebleeds."

"I doubt that, too."

"Can't say that I love them," Shaker says. "The nosebleeds."

"You go to a lot of movies?"

"Nah."

"You read books? Do you have any subscriptions? Have you cultivated a rich interior life?"

"That's why I got a dog."

"I let some men love me," the Howitzer says. "But I'm pretty sure I'm asexual."

"At least you know."

"It's lonely, candy-assed carpet-munchers like yourself that truly sadden me."

"Me too," Shaker says.

"Too much empathy can be a curse." The Howitzer glances around the room with an anxious attention, not taking stock exactly, just roving his overlarge, dreamless head. "Nice place, once you sandblast off the grime."

"You think so?" Shaker asks, a little too desperately.

The Howitzer suckles his thermos, caps it, and begins reeling up the measuring tape he had been stretching around the room when Shaker came home and interrupted him hours ago. The accordion file is on the table, the notebook inside inked with elaborate algorithms, scientific hieroglyphics. Somewhere Shaker found them, stole them, but he's not sure where. His home is embellished with a number of rogue items—dog collars, diaries, bleached bones, gilded trinkets—that mysteriously entered Shaker's possession, all carefully curated yet unexplained. Shaker feels like he is one of these items himself, and so is the Howitzer now. He would like to conclude their friendly ceasefire on an upbeat note, but the hour is late, and old-fashioned hospitality can indeed be a chore.

"You sliced apart the window screen," Shaker blurts. "You crawled in."

The Howitzer scowls, a dismissive shake of his bald head.

Shaker continues anyway. "You tunneled up through the carpet. A trap wall, a hidden chimney. You are astral-projecting yourself onto my crappy futon."

"That would be something, chief."

"I've had worse nightmares."

"This is no nightmare."

"Still," Shaker shrugs, "I've had worse."

Whatever delirium he has tried all night to rebuff or deflect, Shaker has succumbed to it. He rubs his damp shirt into his damp chest. The cold shirt feels more alive than his alive parts do. The Howitzer packs up his tape with his thermos and electric stud finder and stun gun and caffeine pills. "Been missing you down at the Beagle." He says this with a gentle yet firm stare.

"I miss it, too," Shaker says. "The barstool oracles. Bums sleeping in the bathroom. Christmas carols in the middle of July."

"Stop over and see us one of these nights. We'll screw a few on."

"So I won't get clubbed to death?"

"I didn't say that," the Howitzer replies.

There is some early sun tinting the landscape orange, its pocks and folds. Shaker finds little solace in the glow.

He watches the Howitzer plod out the door to the bulky motorcycle aslant on its kickstand. The bald bouncer walks the machine down to the road before revving it awake. Shaker shuts the door and waits, wants to wait, tries waiting. But he's already on his feet and inspecting the windows, the locks, the cabinets, his runaway furniture, his sock drawer, his socks. Shaker sprawls face-down on his mattress for ten agonizing minutes before getting up and auditing it all again.

*

Shaker has taken the Tully truck with the understanding that for every hour he uses the vehicle, he will dedicate an equivalent hour to slathering their house with primer, then painting over the primer, and probably touching up the paint. So he drives, thankful to be liberated from the Hooster girl's bike. He's steering with more care than usual. A shoebox of cassettes rests on the dashboard. Shaker turns on the stereo, and there's already a tape inside: a bootleg recorded straight off the soundboard. Everything is glossed, the drums and organ large in the mix. The band is all session players, very suave on the ligature, but they lack voltage, throttle, a cardinal sin. The recording isn't a show. It's a show's soundcheck. The same song staggers along, stops, restarts, rife with jazzy improv and jocular banter, jarred by the occasional sour chord. Shaker recognizes the chord, the song. He ejects the tape just before her voice booms through the sheen. He chunks the bootleg into the backseat and rummages the shoebox for another tape, but all the tapes are boot-legs, and all of them contain his ex-wife, her schizo-phrenic incarnations, and the anonymous men in crisp suits and slick hair who backed them. He squints at the handwritten label on the side of the shoebox: *The Great American Suction*. He pulls over, places the shoebox on the ground, and rolls the truck over it several times, then resumes driving.

Shaker has no destination at all. He's just driving, driving, watching himself driving.

*

"You jerk."

"Me?" asks Shaker.

"My lotion!"

"Lotion," Shaker replies, barely a foot onto his porch before the girl interrupts his outdoor vodka excursion. She's listing on a hip and stabbing a fuchsia fingernail into his paunch.

"I left it out here, and some jerk has been wasting it. Look." She shakes the bottle into his face. "Empty!"

"Maybe it evaporates."

"Mama seen you out here slicking yourself all over." The girl leans in. She sniffs Shaker down and up. "You smell like my apricots!"

"I work in the sun," Shaker shrugs. "And I like apricots."

"*Gawd.*"

"I'll buy you more. A lifetime supply. Just let me have my vodka in peace."

The girl glances at the empty bottle with its crusted spout and gives it a sharp, concluding squeeze.

"Listen," says Shaker. "Not all of us can lambast our way so smoothly across the tundra."

"What's that even *mean?*"

Shaker stares at her blankly.

"Does it have to mean something?" he asks.

"You are such a frivolous dude."

"Frivolous?"

"Yeah. It's a word."

45

"Someone has improved the water pressure on my shower nozzle. They swept my floors and took out my trash. They're trying to drive me crazy."

"Speaking of driving." The girl tosses the bottle and crosses her arms. "Have you seen what happened to my bike? My beautiful, mangled, broken damn bike?"

*

A long day on his machine has reduced Shaker to a genteel cast. He feels slack and accommodating as he ramps his mower and straps it on the flatbed with bungee rope, a canvas tarp. Hob and Munk and Arnold and Flander are gathering the hacksaws and pruning shears from their triage area around a sick elm. Thin unbuckles himself from his Weed Eater and bags the lengthy contraption in a duffel that's almost his own height. Shaker watches him stealthily while pretending to double-check the flatbed fasteners, the knots and pulleys and locks. Shaker no longer wears that wonderful apricot smell his coworkers have been snickering about, but his tan is near-golden. He is maintaining a glorious pair of mutton-chop sideburns. His nerves are mostly intact. After Thin has dragged the sacked contraption onto the flatbed and weighted it in place with another duffel full of tools, Shaker removes the bandanna from his forehead and wrings the sweat and says, "You were right."

"Was I," says Thin.

"The Tullys. They're bum news. My mistake."

"Of course it was your mistake. Just like that jungle gym." Thin points to the titanium skeleton that Shaker accidentally strafed with his side bumper not one hour ago. The play equipment now leans too prominently to the left.

"Careless, I guess," Shaker says.

"I'm seeing contrails," whispers Thin.

"Pardon?"

"Everywhere, man. Streaks and halos. Sunsets and controlled burns. I'm popping pills by the fistful, and I'm still weed-whacking my shit straight."

"You are that good."

Thin has his thumbs hooked over his trouser waistband, deputy style.

"So you really done with Tullys."

"I am," Shaker says.

Thin takes a lazy yawn and arches an eyebrow. "This mean you're partying?"

Shaker mimics the yawn and says, "Maybe."

"Well, the *maybe* truck is gassed to the *maybe* brim and about to pull the *maybe* fuck out," Thin replies, but Shaker is already scrambling into the middle seat.

The party site is not a ramshackle cabin or double-wide trailer as Shaker expects, but rather a two-story Greek Revival with garage and porch and tire-swing in the backyard. Shaker follows Thin and Munk into a cathedral foyer that culminates in an arched window of stained glass, kaleidoscopic colors filtered around the staircase and walls. Shaker shambles along, dazed by the surreal palette. He enters the kitchen where Roderick Bartholomew is already at work, breaking apart a brown brick.

"Cap'n Bartholomew took a personal day," Thin tells Shaker. "Prep time, you understand? Plus expenses."

Thin's hand is extended in anticipation. Shaker self-consciously inspects his own hands, noting a fine crescent of black gunk under each fingernail. Then he realizes he's being solicited. He tweezes a twenty from his wallet and tries not to visibly wince as he forks it over. A whole week in grocery funds.

"Danke," says Thin. "Make yourself at home."

"Where's the pisser in this place?" Shaker asks.

Thin spins around the kitchen, innocently perplexed, like a young tourist who has strayed too far from his hostel. "Anybody know where el baño is at?"

"Negative," Roderick murmurs as he sorts through a collection of razor blades fanned across the granite countertop. He selects one, tests it on his thumb cuticle, and begins slicing the brown mound in surgical increments. "Minnesotan is locked in the attic. Dude was spooking me so much I couldn't concentrate on Sargent Rock here."

Thin looks at Shaker and shrugs. "Happy hunting."

Shaker wanders back to the foyer and ascends the staircase, blinking at all the wild peacock colors, and tours the unfurnished upstairs. Bathroom, bedrooms, closets, all empty. The only indication of human life is the footfalls and squashy thumps from the attic. The Minnesotan—who is, in fact, a seventh-generation Ohioan—has long maintained a fabled reputation among the local community of huffers, snuffers, dullards, and ne'er-do-wells. Shaker has witnessed the man stumble through a rich array of social milieus and wilt rather splendidly in each of them. But Shaker can't remember ever once seeing him open his mouth and actually speak.

Shaker finds no papers to rummage, no trunks to ransack. He enters a nice, wide room and urinates in the middle of it. He hops over the briny lake of effluent, already starting to stink, and inscribes his initials in a dusty windowpane, then heads down the staircase. Munk meets him in the foyer, squinting up through the religious sunlight, a sack of kitty litter under each arm.

"Hey, new guy," says Munk. "Gimme a hand."

Shaker grabs a bag. "I've been on that machine all summer. What's new about that?"

"New guy always gets put on the machine. Working with clippers and rakes and spades, those are professional hallmarks."

"Hallmarks," Shaker nods.

"Look at me, son. I am an artisan with an artisan's hands. Touch them."

Shaker looks at the hands. Plenty of black gunk. Shaker hefts his bag as if it's lighter than it really is and carries it past the kitchen to an alcove in the darkened den, where the drug squatters have relocated. Thin and Roderick and Flander and two people Shaker doesn't recognize are hunched around a table. On the table is a fish. The two strangers are operating a large bicycle pump/bong hybrid, one pumping it, the other inserting its transparent tube into the fish's mouth. The fish is spiny, zebra-colored, and it inflates to light-bulb size.

"Okay," one says. "Quick quick quick."

Thin, sliding on a pair of robust metalworker gloves, grabs the fish and holds it at nipple level, tilts down his head, and he simultaneously squeezes the sea creature and sucks its smoky, juicy output. His pale face is clenched, his arm shaking. The men all unleash a festive football cheer while Shaker stares, his own stomach in a grotesque torque.

"Well?" Thin gasps, his face brick red, handing the fish and glove to Shaker. "You partying or not?"

Two days later, Shaker is still trying to get home, schlepping the same strip of churned gravel again and again, facial muscles in frantic conniption, searching for his shoes and socks. The undersides of his feet are blistered and inscrutable as artichokes. The black gunk is prevailing. His shoes and his socks are somewhere along this dark and dirty road. He knows they are.

His teeth will not stop humming.

When Shaker was a schoolboy and first asked for a dog, his mother sighed theatrically, set her perennial wineglass aside, and sat her son on her knee. "I asked for a puppy, too, when I was your age," she told him. "A boxy-faced Schnauzer that was uniquely coarse-haired and spritely and even in its best moments carried a strong smell of liverwurst. The first day out of the crate, it ran off the porch and bit the milkman. We had milkmen in those days, dear. Real bastions of civic integrity. The milkman sued us for the dog bite, and my parents countersued because he wasn't technically *our* milkman, he was our neighbor's milkman. We may have also sued the neighbor. The municipality got involved because the puppy wasn't licensed, and the code-enforcement gestapo intervened because half our land fell outside the city line and was only zoned for livestock and poultry. At some point, my parents hired a private investigator, although for the life of me I can't remember why. There's no happy ending to this story. The boy wants a puppy, he will have a puppy." She pinched a small piece of Shaker's young cheek. "But the moment you take your eyes off that dog, I will let it off its leash, open the front gate, sit back, and watch the fireworks unfold. Because life is all about the little lessons."

Some nights, Shaker rants so loud in his sleep, he awakes with a bruised throat. For a long time, he wondered what he was saying, so he borrowed a tape recorder and clip mic and tacked together an ad hoc system to monitor his slumber sounds. It took him several attempts, but he did capture one of these nocturnal monologues. It consisted of a single word, repeated over and over, like a sacred mantra: *Shaker, Shaker, Shaker, Shaker.*

Shaker smashed the tape recorder and burned the tape and began sleeping with a clean washcloth crammed in his mouth.

This morning, he is hoarse again. He takes his time in the bathroom, gargling mouthwash and salt water and dribbling most of it on the floor. Then he enjoys a modest breakfast of stale cereal and three slices of wheat toast charred so horrifically unrecognizable they require forensic identification. He scarfs down his breakfast while standing in his front room, looking through the window at the Tully truck. Shaker has lost track of the hours he owes. He has convinced himself that extended possession of the vehicle now obligates him to a thorough wash/wax/towel-buff session, which he inevitably delays, too. And so the truck sits, frozen and pointless, an elegy to all Shaker's lingering debts.

There is only one choice of pet store. Avalon Animals is a dark, unsymmetrical affront to retail architecture; there's nothing boxy or bright or antiseptic about it. The fluorescent lights and air conditioning are turned off, yet the store is open. Inside, Shaker wanders the long aisles. He tries not to get too distracted by the caged toucans and hermit crab colonies and ferrets siesta'ing in their nylon hammocks, not when what he really wants to visit are the tanked fish. He shuffles up to the wide glass, which is layered with his own ghastly reflection. He pinches his lower lip. Licks his hair into stead. The tank is fishless. Just brackish water and a set of car keys sunk among the bottom pebbles. Shaker approaches the bland, pretty cashier to query her about special orders, baked brains, lost socks. The woman has a loose-hanging face and creamy complexion, her cheek skin so slack a person could basket apples in it. Something about the woman perturbs him. Shaker nods and smiles and rushes out the door without saying anything at all.

At least he is able to competently navigate himself home. Rather than park at the duplex, however, he continues to circle his neighborhood, loop upon loop upon loop, like a recent parolee awed by the restless, golden fields of freedom, looking for something warm and familiar to burgle.

*

This house is a rustic colonial on a county route placed far back among pines and nettles so that, seen from a distance, only the house's gambled rooftop is announced from the green. The men are in the backyard patio area, gathered around a sand-filled bocce ball court. Silently, they stare at the sand, a pensive brood. Some recently smoked puffer fish rests in a swirl of brown juices on the grill. The men, six of them, are utterly transfixed, as if worshiping an ancient and enigmatic shrine.

Shaker has slunk into a hypnotic trance of his own. He's settled among the luau-themed patio equipment, feeling oddly tender as he surveys the scene. Behind a shrub wall, the Minnesotan is spread-eagle on the grass, his face planted in a patch of poison oak. A many-tentacled bicycle-pump bong is coiled like a sea monster on a patio table alongside some blackened glass. Everything seems narcotized and inert in a shoebox diorama type of way. Shaker takes a sip from his canteen and reclines his bamboo-stick chair. Soon he is submerged in a dream terrain of impenetrable suburban fortresses built entirely from PVC conduit and torched Pyrex.

*

When Shaker wakes, his throat is parched and his canteen has vanished. The sun is declining. A boom box blares a dubbed cassette of high-velocity power thrash sung in garbled Paraguayan, and someone has taken a malicious piss in the bocce sand. The urinater possessed both remarkable volume and trajectory, resulting in a dark stain six feet in diameter, a spiral vortex design. Shaker inspects the stain in genuine puzzlement and decides to seek inspiration elsewhere. He looks through the window into the colonial's kitchen. The supply table is collaged with knives and skillet and skin and aquatic guts. Munk is taking deep hits from a plastic pen pressed to a puffer wrapped in tinfoil. Flander assists with the flame. The lit fish changes colors, turquoise-striped to speckled yellow.

Back on the patio, Thin is spazzing his limbs in crazy windmill arcs, unable to dance coherently to the rampaging music. Shaker retracts his legs onto his chair and realizes his feet are naked and cold. His new boots are gone. There is also, vaguely, a tweeze in his arm. Shaker holds up the arm and sees a spiny fish stuck in the soft meat of his elbow. His mouth is numb, his voice box, his face. None of it can yell. Shaker stumbles off the chair, barefoot and terrified, trying to shake off the freaky thing. Only by utilizing a pair of barbecue tongs is he able to successfully detach himself.

The other men are too rapt with their own stupors to commiserate. Shaker returns to his seat, kicks his bare feet back up, and notices a second and third fish dangling from the flab of each thigh. Defeated, he reattaches the original fish to his swollen artery, which he guesses is an aorta of some sort.

After a while, Shaker can't resist. He raises the arm, rotates it slowly in the low tiki light, admiring his new appendage, and that's how he catches sight of the female clerk from the pet store. She is standing in the kitchen, passing a basketful of spiky fish—all of them bagged in gleaming water, like prizes from a boardwalk game—to Roderick, who in turn trades her a clam of cash. The woman recedes from view.

Shaker is already on his feet and stumbling around the side of the house, but he gets snarled in some pine branches. By the time he extracts himself from the foliage and glimpses the woman again, she is disappearing into the passenger side of a damaged hatchback. The calico vehicle's fender is secured via rope and electrician tape, and there is a *Caution: Student Driver* placard in the rear window. An unfamiliar man, slump shouldered, menacing in size, looms at the steering wheel. The car backs down the driveway, going a little crooked across the yard and grazing the curb. And then it is gone.

Roderick is still in the kitchen straining some foul-smelling seawater through a Rube Goldberg filtration system, convoluted tubes and fizzing funnels, all jury-rigged together.

"That piss smells delicious," Shaker says in a slur, still unable to feel his mouth.

"You do not interrupt Michelangelo when he is lying on his back with his private parts mashed against the ceiling, paint oozing in his face."

"I guess not." Shaker gagging on the nautical stench. "Unless you are offering a bribe."

He points to the Tupperware tub of spiky, new deliveries. He tucks a twenty into Roderick's chest pocket.

"You got an aquarium at home?"

"Yes," Shaker says.

Roderick removes the surgical mask from his mouth. "Take the runt. Give it a good home. Do not give it a name. Trust me, man. Never name the thing you plan to someday smoke."

Shaker grabs the runtiest bagged fish and holds it in his cupped hands, peering down at it like a Magic 8-Ball. "Good morning, Junior Shaker," he says, making googly eyes at the purple fish.

*

The pet store is closed and the parking lot empty, and Shaker still insists on occupying the sole handicap spot. He can't explain his compulsion to drive back here. Maybe some simpatico toxin is still working its way around his bloodstream. Maybe he just needs a quiet place to rest. He sets Junior Shaker on the dashboard and watches the fish twirl in its big bag. Then he watches the homeless men and women across the highway. There is a whole encampment of them established on this flat parcel of rural roadside: sheets hung from tree limbs, fire pits, cardboard slabs tilted into huts. Shaker is fascinated by the industrious nomads who are not beholden. They have rearticulated the lie at the root of the frontier myth. Shaker thinks about visiting their shantytown for a few hours, sharing the homemade libations they have concocted from stale fruit and crusted gym socks, roasting varmint meat on sticks. But he just watches the show instead. His knee judders on the lifeless stereo console. He talks sporadically to his fish. Sleep comes in fits and starts and the starts of fits.

When he wakes the next morning, the sun is sautéing him through the windshield and the truck's temperature has risen to near-volcanic levels. Shaker, slantwise on the rear seat, finds his cheek is adhered to the hot vinyl with a clump of dried drool. He digs under the cushion and discovers an expired credit card that he uses to chisel his face free. Simultaneously, a random idea is jostled loose: Shaker doesn't own an aquarium at home. He has no large container or backyard pond—not even a decent-size pretzel bowl—to lodge the fish. But it doesn't matter. Shaker cranks down the window to let in some ambient breeze. He fans the air with his hands to no effect. Junior Shaker is still resting on the dashboard in his shiny plastic bag, magnified in hellish sunlight, and no longer purple.

The puffer is not only dead. The blameless little guy has been poached white as an egg.

Shaker tries not to think about it. This time he uses the bunk credit card to scrape the skin off the pale corpse. At first, the scales peel easily, but Shaker is too zealous with his technique, and soon he is frantically grating the puffer like a hunk of Parmesan cheese. Shaker stuffs the skin shreds in the ashtray and plops the meat in his mouth. He swallows the evidence in a single, dutiful gulp.

"That wasn't so awful," he tells the reflection in the rearview mirror, a sweat-frazzled and disheveled man, lacking imagination and moral authority, who does not seem to believe him.

Then Shaker drives home, cozies up with the toilet, and voids his stomach for days.

6.

Once a month, the Brothers Tully host militia training maneuvers in and around the thirty-odd acres that entrench their house. Since Shaker owes the Brothers approximately a full week's labor for use of their truck, he has been conscripted into service this Sunday afternoon. The game is paintball, and he joins the angry secessionists and meth mummies and paroled vagrants who have also been coaxed through assorted Tully-related obligation. Shaker is kitted up in camouflage and fourthhand hockey pads, humping things into position. Thanks to the dearth in available head armor, he can see a few exposed faces that he recognizes. Stool slouchers from the Beagle, grocery stockers, an alderman, a Shriner. Even Bob Mossenfeld, who managed the only used auto lot in town and sold Shaker his old van before he was fired for lagging odometers. The Minnesotan sits with a shotgun cracked open on its hinge. He's trying to huff the paint cartridge inside. Hunkered on another tree stump is Bitters McCaulky. The reverend's face is clamped with concentration as he velcros on his body-molded shin guards and aluminum crotch shield. He's suiting up for some serious castle siege. Shaker hurriedly crams his head into his ski mask. Then he straightens his bullet belt and thermal gloves, his night-vision goggles although it is not night. Fully pieced together, he walks up and holds his gun point-blank to McCaulky's cheek and gives the trigger a dainty pinch. A loud lisp of compressed air. The man's head jerks. Red paint decorates all immediate parties. Shaker thinks he can read in the spatter the cryptic intimations of his own existential liberation. It more or less resembles red velvet cake.

"Bombs away," Shaker says and returns to his team of junky addicts and lonely stalkers and school board members. A Tully blows a bullhorn.

The skirmish can now officially begin.

*

Shaker spends his night alone on the patio, serenaded by the baying of mongrel dogs. As much as he enjoys the dogs' company, the animals have always been too afraid to approach him. He is bundled in gabardine against the high breezes, pretending the footsteps he hears indoors are only the Hooster woman and girl kicking with agitation over the most recent news. Their radio is dialed to a local station running breathless coverage of a string of recent B&E violations in which the homeowners were found bound with bungee rope and bent over sofas, socks stuffed in mouth, cucumbers wedged in their nether territories. There are rumors of lubrication trails, surveillance traps, psychic crime-solvers trekking in from downstate. Shaker has no firsthand knowledge of these incidents, but he feels confident he could play the role of "flummoxed bystander interviewed by regional cable TV affiliate" if given the opportunity. He has only made one significant media appearance over the years. The weekly pennysaver ran a photo of Shaker performing on stage at a county fair. He had a vicious lip sneer, his legs fixed in classic rock-and-roll straddle, his instrument very visibly unplugged. *Who's On First Bass?* ran the headline. Shaker clipped the photo anyway and keeps it in a manila envelope taped to the bottom of his futon mattress.

He has no such documentation, however, of the mysterious sleepwalking sprees that were his other public humiliation in that era. Shaker would fall asleep in his bed like any other semi-lucid civilian, only to regain consciousness hours later—ten or fifteen miles from his house—standing barefoot in convenience store aisles, fast-food drive-thrus, the garages of startled residents. These long somnambular jaunts would leave his mental faculties a little moiled and his shanks sore for days. But Shaker's foremost regret is he never learned where he was trying to go, if he had any tangible destination at all.

He rises from his beach chair to raid his secret vodka reserve in the refrigerator meat drawer, but he can't quite see the meat drawer, not exactly, not with all this fresh fluid suddenly rising into his eyes. Some galactic compression is squeezing the drunk and sentimental juices right out of him. So Shaker swings into the bathroom and fumbles for the faucet, hoping cold water will shock the sadness away. The water will only run hot. So hot it scalds. He checks the showerhead, the kitchen faucet, the spigot outside. Same and same and same.

"Bombs away," he mutters at the mirror, the steamy splotch that once was his sweet, innocent face.

*

The mower is overturned in the yard with its grass-gunked underbelly exposed while Shaker prepares to replace the five-foot-long machete that is the machine's rotary blade. The old blade is dinged badly and cuts uneven, a result of Shaker skimming a water sprinkler that stubbornly had not retracted into its hole. Shaker whips the bad blade sideward like a scythe, hooking weeds and hacking them, and then he stabs it in the dirt and starts tearing the replacement out of its plastic sheath.

The orange cottage and its fence and shed are the only structures mounted on this small hill, and the wind rams them at all angles. The sky appears to rain pebbles and grit. Black stockings ripple and kick like ghostly showgirls on a clothesline. There is a herd of feral cats under the porch, and their eyes are gleaming through the scrim of darkness like polished nickels.

Shaker's surgery on the machine progresses slowly. He smells ripe in all this toil and sunlight. For three days, he has been unable to shower at home, and the reek is untenable. He holds his shirt over his nose as he works. He reminds himself that in Europe natural stink is the fashion. After the blade is replaced and the shrapnel cleaned up, Shaker approaches the cottage at a casual saunter. Thin and Hob Brock and a heavyset migrant named Mach Whatever are assailing an invasive stack of hedges on the side yard. The migrant's radio is broadcasting reggae rock. The song is mild and rubber-limbed and makes the afternoon labor feel leisurely and festive. Shaker strolls onto the porch. He knocks, listens, knocks again, and with a blasé shrug he rears back on his heels. Nobody is watching him. Even the cats are quiet. The door pushes open easily. It wasn't locked at all. Shaker gives one last look over his shoulder before slinking inside.

*

Shaker's leg feels the high winds coming. That limb, and Shaker with it, had been run over and improperly repaired the previous year, and now, in his only clairvoyant talent, it can gauge the approach of inclement weather. Six pins in all. He had been hazed on drink and muscle relaxants that night and was waiting in front of the Regal Beagle for his cousin to bring around the car. Darb overshot the sidewalk, accelerated backwards too hastily, and ran Shaker down. For more than an hour, Shaker was trapped under Doris's rust-clung Skylark, his leg mangled, a steady stream of antifreeze piddling in his face as the drugs slowly rubbed off. That's when Shaker, gazing up into a stretch of dark hose, had the thought. He envisioned himself stranded under the vehicle for weeks and months, centuries and millennia, as teenage delivery boys continued to bring him emergency pizzas, his magazine subscriptions got rerouted, his sex organ shriveled, and a platoon of comely dental hygienists paid him periodic visits. And just how alluring that all sounded.

Today, the wind catches him at the right angle. Sensation runs up his leg and disperses across the tiny rods and nuts that scaffold his kneecap. And Shaker can't help it, the thought returns, solid and unmovable, colonizing all that deserted real estate in his mind.

Accident or not, a man's ability to abide could be his own undoing.

*

In another week, Hob Brock pulls him off his machine shortly after lunch. Shaker has half the new lawn cut in crop circle patterns and nonsensical symbols, an enigmatic mess he intended to fully raze on a second pass, but he grew too maudlin about his patterns, too devotional. Now the mower is shut off, and the grass remains mystifyingly butchered. Shaker is only marginally abashed. Hob takes him by the elbow and walks him to some nearby shade.

"Sit with me, Shaker."

Shaker sits with him.

"Ms. Blaudin." Hob points at the clapboard cottage. "That woman's been living here ninety-three years. I know because when I was a punk kid we used to harass this house, roll it with toilet paper, pelt it with rotten eggs, crap on its porch, blare our stupid music. The shit kids do, Shaker. It disgusts me at my age, but I understand it. And I bet Ms. Blaudin understands it as well. That woman has seen a lot of dimwitted history in her tenure. She's been bombarded. But I'm willing to bet in all her years in that adorable orange cottage, she's never had a yard boy waltz through the front door and soak himself in her claw-foot tub during his lunch break."

Shaker turns quizzical.

"The tub had claw feet?" he asks.

Hob has an arm around Shaker. The man's spicy musk is mingling with the gasoline Shaker has been harboring in his lungs all week. He may have ruptured a fuel line on that sprinkler nozzle. But it does feel good to be bathing daily again.

Hob gives Shaker a brotherly squeeze and says, "How about after we finish this yard, you and me go have a drink in honor of our good friend Shaker's early retirement."

The sun is slanting through the trees, the tree shadows slanting in tandem. Shaker is overwhelmed by the urge to lean along with them, but he knows the sun and shadows have already cut him loose, too. He turns back to Hob.

"I'd like that very much," he says.

*

The two men are reclined atop the roof of the aluminum shed that contains their mowing equipage. The view is other sheds and warehouses in tidy assembly, a field of crimped tin. October is almost gone. Shaker and Hob sag into their broken lawn chairs, chilled by the air that Shaker surmises is hitting them harder at this altitude. He can feel the nosebleed before it starts. He regrets not wearing a coat to work, a parka, a blindfold. The altitude intimidates him. Beside his chair is a bucket of warm lager, courtesy of Hob. Shaker sips slow and keeps his vision fixed on all that twinkling tin ahead of him, a tissue twisted in his nostril.

"I bet the reception here is astounding," Shaker says.

"Maybe we bring up a TV, a sofa, pretzels in a bowl."

"Sports bar," Shaker nods. "I pawned my set a year ago. I miss the noise. That jolly, ravenous box. Radio seems too ghoulish to me now. Like eavesdropping on the séances of strangers."

Hob drains a bottle and asks, "You fixed for rent?"

"I'm not fixed for anything," Shaker says.

"Then have another beer."

"You drink up here often?"

"My secret spot. It is refreshingly human-and-bullshit free."

"The extra elevation probably gets you lit quicker."

"I take what I can get. And I know you do, too, bathtub moocher."

Shaker smiles at this and crosses his legs, an overweening sort of pose.

"My synapses are a little loose," he says.

"They *look* loose."

"Maybe I drag some blankets up here, spend the night."

"This is my shed, man. If I wanted to run a bed-and-breakfast, I'd move to Vermont."

"Vermont's a little far for me," Shaker says.

"You're too spooked to be in your own home."

"Spooked isn't the word."

"Spooked is *exactly* the word," Hob replies. "And please uncross your legs, dude. There are neighbors."

When Shaker sighs, the breath squeezed through his gapped teeth sounds like an asthmatic kazoo. "It was a solid crew."

"They're burnouts and bums and fiends. I know this."

"Just being cordial."

"Fuck cordial," says Hob. "Cordial never saved anybody's ass in the trench."

"These beers, this siesta."

"What about?"

"This isn't cordial?"

"Shit," Hob says. His bottle is empty, but he's itching the label, his fingernails tacky with glue residue. He raises the bottle and pitches it overboard, grimacing at the broad arc of glass that neatly approximates the earth's curvature. Hob's expression stays stiff, pasted, as the bottle smashes beyond view.

"Who gets moved to the mower?" Shaker asks.

"It's just a machine, man."

"I know."

"Flander will ride the thing until he kills somebody. Only a month of work left anyway."

"Maybe I can broker something with the Tullys. Score some shovel-and-salt work for us."

"Do not get me mixed up with those black-market gun nuts. And remember, you are retired."

"Vermont awaits," Shaker says.

Hob dredges another bottle from the bucket and fits it into Shaker's hand. "Jesus, you do make the citizens nervous, Shaker."

"Something about my head." Shaker points at the bloody tissue.

"That's right," Hob says. "That's very, very right."

64

*

Three o'clock in the morning and Shaker is fully freighted with drink. The room has stopped spinning, but he's still digging his hocks in the rug, establishing temporary traction in case the carousel resumes. The crowbar is in his lap. He sees it but doesn't feel it. My contours, Shaker thinks. I do not fit my own contours. He looks up. The Howitzer crowds the doorway in his unzipped windbreaker and Beagle Staff shirt, skin bronzed, a neon lanyard full of keys hung around his beefy neck. He has removed his ivory moccasins, and Shaker admires the manicured toenails that accessorize the bouncer's feet. The Howitzer fastens each shoe on a shoe-tree branch and activates a few more lamps and sits across from Shaker in a leather recliner that has brew holders built into the posh arms, an electronic control panel, digital hi-fi. The man seems to Shaker a small nation of tranquility.

"I didn't need it," Shaker says, indicating the crowbar. "Your window was unlocked."

"Silent alarm."

"Okay," Shaker nods.

"I already called the cops, told them not to bother. Just a confused fawn wandering in lost from the forest. So I shot it. They applauded my initiative and stellar marksmanship. I knew you'd do something foolish eventually."

Shaker requests the Howitzer move to the center of the room. The Howitzer sighs and reluctantly rises. He stands there on the rug examining the pink wicks of his fingernails as Shaker leaps from his rocking chair and slams into the Howitzer's chest. The unsuccessful tackle more and more resembles a desperate hug the longer

Shaker stays latched around the Howitzer's middle, as if still clinging to the slender notion of vengeance itself.

"You got any beer in this cabana?" Shaker asks, face nuzzled in the Howitzer's stomach.

"Smells like you've already hit your quota. How about something from the tap?"

"Only if it's a thousand goddamn degrees."

"Easy, chief," the Howitzer says. He detaches himself from Shaker and returns with a glass of water. Shaker sits and accepts the drink with a vulgar gesture he immediately regrets. The Howitzer remains standing, a geometry of skis and poles racked over his head. They very nearly resemble antlers.

Shaker takes a prolonged sip and says, "Because I can't get any sleep in my own fucking Winnebago."

"That's probably the point."

Shaker studies the sweaty glass, unsure if the sweat is his or the tap water's.

"I know that," he says. "I know that's the point."

"You're not the only one suffering here. Waking up at odd hours, stumbling around your place in the dark, finding new and inventive ways to unravel you. That crappy little duplex depresses me, chief."

"I always liked it."

"That depresses me, too," the Howitzer says.

Shaker holds the wet glass to his forehead, rolling his attention from one Howitzer foot to the other. Big, pulpy bricks. The man must need special sneakers. He must shop in special stores. Shaker imagines the Howitzer as an awkward teenager, sulking out of all the usual franchise chains at the only local mall, mocked by slobbish salespeople, his monstrous feet sore in too-small shoes.

"Is that nail polish?"

The Howitzer gently lifts Shaker's head away from his stumpy toes and aligns it at eye level. "Shaker," he says.

"One day I'd really like to learn the bolero," Shaker says through clenched molars. "Just let me *bolero*."

"Don't you ever wonder why the shitstorm started?"

Shaker can't nod with his head in the Howitzer's hand, so he blinks once, twice, once, a Morse code of facial tic. But even then, he's still not sure his answer.

"I do a special kind of freelance work for people," says the Howitzer. "People who don't like you. If my bank account is any indicator, their numbers are legion."

Shaker twists his mouth, a confused funnel.

"I thought I was a people person," Shaker says.

The Howitzer smiles tiredly and takes the glass from Shaker. "You can stop blinking now."

"Viva," Shaker replies and pretends to lift an imaginary glass. The pantomime feels heavier than the real thing.

"As much as I'd like to stay up for the slumber party, I need sleep," the Howitzer says. "Gotta get up early tomorrow morning to disconnect the heat at your house."

Shaker nods slowly. "I'm sure I have some errands, too."

He rises and steadies and is aiming for the door when he begins patting his pants, his shirt pocket.

"Think I lost my house key," he mumbles. "Must've bounced from my pocket when I shimmied off the shed."

"You think I have a spare," says the Howitzer.

Shaker shrugs. "You're getting in somehow."

The Howitzer reaches around Shaker and opens the door, then stands with his arms folded, refusing to budge that great, meaty mound of a head. He gives a rugged smirk and slides a key off his neon lanyard's ring.

"Gracias," Shaker says, pocketing the duplicate.

"No problem," the Howitzer tells him. "But I'm gonna need that back tomorrow morning."

*

Still, even more mysteriously, Shaker cannot continue inside. He loiters under a sputter of starlight on the yard, feeling tedious, unawake. There is sitcom chatter on the Hooster half, television voices, and the canned laughter seems aimed directly at the character Shaker has been duped into playing. An insomniac is running a vacuum somewhere. Someone is sending a casserole through a paper shredder. Shaker has slipped off his shoes and is rubbing his toes in the crisp sod. His windows are dark, all dark. He can almost imagine his indoor self framed and illuminated against those black squares, a restless animal in exhibit, oblivious to any audience. But he can't quite see the look of stunned witlessness on his usual face.

"You locked your idiot self out?"

The Hooster girl is at her window, TV gibbering behind her. Shaker holds up the copied key. "I'm admiring the view."

"And?"

"Needs more crop circles. Maybe a tiki torch or two."

"I thought you were that guy," the girl says. "The fix-it guy with the weird hours."

"I'm him tonight. How's your water? Your heat?"

"Normal. Unlike you."

"He'll be back tomorrow."

"He helped me fix up the bike you broke."

"I didn't break it," Shaker says.

"It's not meant to be rode on by drunk, old, idiot jerks. He got me a new chain and unbent the banana seat and even put on pink reflectors for free."

"He's a good specimen."

The Hooster girl nods.

"Am I?" Shaker asks.

"Are you what?"

"A good specimen."

Shaker shifts uneasily, fumbles a shoe.

"You alright out there?" the girl asks.

Shaker kneads his jaw until he hears the tired bone click.

7.

Truckless today, Shaker tramps to the grocery store on foot. He doesn't have enough funds to purchase anything, but he enjoys wandering the glossy, checkered aisles of modern commerce on his day off, aloof and hungry, maybe shoplifting a vittle or two. *All* his days are days off now. Shaker is en route on the roadside, not leaning far into traffic, when he is almost guillotined by a passing car's side mirror. The car swerves belatedly and pulls onto the shoulder to wait for him. Shaker recognizes the vehicle—its duct-taped fender dangling like a ragged hangnail—from the puffer party. In daylight, he gets a better look. The exterior is glamorized with ritzy window tint and chrome hubs and gaudy trim that fail to offset the vehicle's general dilapidation. The woman clerk climbs out the passenger door. She smiles blandly at Shaker, then points inside the car. Shaker feigns a flinty indifference, dips his head, and peers inside.

His cousin is staring back at him from the driver's seat. Someone has prepared Darb in a handsome sweater vest and color-coordinated chinos. All the life-sick wrinkles seem to have been steam-pressed from his narrow, untroubled face.

"Long time, no parlez-vous," Darb says brightly. "Want a ride? You are a rough goddamn sight, cousin. A *rough* sight."

Shaker's leggy frame is accordioned in the backseat, his gaze shifting from Darb's head to the woman's head to Darb's head again. He can't catch much of their faces in the rearview mirror, but he can hear Darb's plastic dentures clacking with every bounce and jolt of the car. The whole vehicle interior smells like cinnamon napalm and canned tuna. The woman sits silently with a Tupperware full of puffers hugged in her lap.

"Making deliveries?" Shaker asks.

"The wonders of oceanography." Darb gives the woman's trove a courtly pat. He follows Shaker's gaze and says, "You remember Lorelei?"

"I do not."

"It's a funny story," Darb says, noisily chewing his dentures, and then he stops talking altogether.

Shaker tries to reach around to shake Lorelei's hand but has trouble negotiating the seat angle. He reaches his other arm around, flopping both at her. The overall impression, he fears, is that he is threatening to Heimlich the poor woman. She brushes his knuckles and whispers hello. Shaker withdraws the arms without additional comment or intrusion.

They drive the rest of the route in silence. The car curves off the road and down a hidden driveway to a southwestern ranch home, low and long, with stucco coating and terracotta roof tiles. Lorelei is abruptly gone into the garage. Shaker and Darb remain in the hatchback with the engine cut, listening to the vehicle's ruptured head gasket settle and dribble and steam.

"What do you think, man?" Darb asks. "Surprised?"

"You're her chauffeur. Her butler."

"Try again."

"Drug gopher?"

Darb sighs and twists around, his seatbelt wrapping him at the neck.

"We found each other a month ago. Total accident. I was at the pet store to stock up on my munchies, my snacks. Brought a few dozen cat food tins to the register, and there she was. Hadn't seen each other in years, man. The two of us had a romantic thing in one of our rehabs. Back then, I was doing all that shoe polish. She was snorting pixie sticks. Cousin, we had our nasal cavities so badly augered we couldn't even smell *smell*. Got busy a few times. Apparently, life got a lot busier nine months after I checked out."

"Oh no."

"I'm a daddy!" Darb yelps, throwing a few rabbit punches at the air. "And a damn fine one, too! The boy is maybe a little retarded in some social office, but these days that's how true genius is rolled. That kind of oddity wins the big prizes. And maybe that's a little of me, also. You should see us together. It's a ghastly performance, but I'm trying."

Shaker can almost smell the singe and smoke of a dozen blown fuses somewhere in his own head. He catches his baffled glare in the window. Blinks disinterestedly at it.

"Don't you think I'd be a good daddy, Shakes? My old man suffered black moods so corrupt he ran off before I ever met him. I can't do a worse job than that. This is a whole new level of adult responsibility, and I'm stepping up. The hounds have been called indoors to account."

"Puffer fish," Shaker says.

"Blowfish, actually."

"What's the difference?"

"We're rebranding," Darb tells him. "People hear the word *puffer* and find it sorta distasteful. Not sure why.

Blowfish has a lascivious connotation, too, but it plays well with our target demos. Me and Lorelei handle the entrepreneurial stuff. Arrangements. Facilitation."

"Oceanography," Shaker nods.

Darb smiles crookedly and says, "It's legit, man. Nothing too illegal, at least nothing serious. A little book-cooking at the store is all. These blowfish are outrageous. They got this hidden toxin, you see, and if you take it in just the right dose it stuns the shit out of you, makes you trippy, sublime. You watch the nature channel shows? Dolphins get high off the little buggers and then bob on the ocean surface for hours, laughing at their own reflections, all loopy and whatnot. And everyone knows how whiz-clever dolphins are. The only trick is humans can't take too much or it'll numb you into a coma, maybe kill you. The risks of skipping carelessly through the golden gates of Shangri-La, I guess. Also, you gotta be careful the blowfish don't blow up."

"When you say *blow up*—"

"Like, uh, *explode*. Basically, we got a full-on distillery happening here. Extractions and expanders and all sorts of filters and crap. We're pioneers! Just as long as PETA doesn't catch wind, a dude like me could live like a middle-class citizen for once, provide for his loved ones, and so on. I'm trying to accrue a life here, compadre."

"We are not so many miles from the Yarn Barn," Shaker says. "Are we?"

Darb meets him with a steely stare, the cords in his neck round and tense. Shaker mumbles an apology and Darb chuckles, slides his head out of its seatbelt noose, and slaps Shaker's leg.

"Wanna go inside? Eat some supper? See the freak show?"

The front yard is girded by lank trees on all sides. A basketball hoop leans off its post in the driveway. In the backyard, Shaker glimpses the beginnings of a trampoline, half a hammock, a badminton net obscured by unfinished fence.

"My projects," Darb says. "Idle hands, etceteras."

When he's finished flapping his arms, he leads Shaker around the garage. Shaker pauses at a window and peers in. The space is painted various shades of salmon and lit by floor lamps and incense candles. Lorelei sits on a yoga mat among a battery of mothballed aerobics machinery, her thin body bent into a kind of human bowl, vaguely sculptural. All her parts appear to be vibrating at once. Shaker steps away from the window and turns his attention to the basketball net, the trees, the yard.

"Is this what happiness smells like?" he asks.

"I can't whiff jack-shit anymore." Darb shrugs and taps his nostrils. "The consequence of a life done at full tilt."

"The kid play ball?"

"Wha?" Darb asks.

"Basketball." Shaker points.

"Uh, sure. I mean, you know. It's *there*."

"It *is* there," Shaker agrees.

After a pause, Darb sighs. "The tour continues."

The house is scantly furnished. Pastel walls, tapestries in mellow hues, no tables or chairs, no TV. Shaker feels as if he's strolling an abandoned medical ward or some modernist museum in the Californian mold. He carefully steps over a bead rug on the kitchen floor that has been dressed with finger bowls and chopsticks. In the rec room is the house's only sofa, which Darb regards from the doorway with a sly grin. The room is otherwise empty, and the couch addresses a blank wall. Shaker inspects its leather cushions. He can make out the pronounced dimples of his cousin's rump bone, interred there, a lonely fossil.

"This place is almost as barren as mine," Shaker says, not light on daze.

"It's that austere look. That's the true style. Sheerness, utility. Lorelei's got this Buddha-type philosophy she's introducing me to, along with the granola therapy diets. Can't say I buy it all, but it keeps her feng-shui quotient from freaking the fuck out."

"Guess the rehab calmed her."

Darb conducts a violent semaphore with his hands.

"Hush that shit, man! We don't talk about those days. Especially not near the boy. What happens in Tuscaloosa stays in Tuscaloosa."

"Alabama?"

"Lorelei grew up there. She has shared stories. Gory stuff. Makes Vegas sound like the Vatican."

"Is she gonna eat supper with us?"

"Lorelei?"

"Who else?" Shaker says.

Darb fidgets in the doorway, grabbing fistfuls of chino, his bottom jaw—the real one—distended into an incongruous pout.

"Wanna see the trampoline?" he asks.

After admiring the view of the half-built trampoline frame and ailing bonsai garden and other partially cobbled projects, all refracted by the opaque glass that enfolds the kitchen like a greenhouse, Shaker and Darb hover at the bedroom threshold. The room is all white, a static cube, with scattered candles on the ground and a narrow cot that only sleeps one.

"Tight quarters," says Shaker.

"You mean the bed?"

"More like a cot."

"Sorta. Sorta like a cot."

"Doesn't even look like you'd fit."

Darb uses one hand to hold his head, the other to point down the hall at the rec room couch.

"You sleep on that thing out there?" Shaker asks.

"We're staving off carnal relations until the marriage is official. Keeping things pure, robustly hearted. It's kinda sweet when you think about it."

"So you do a lot of..."

Shaker gesticulates a vigorous two-handed masturbation.

"Like I said, I keep busy. My projects. Check it out."

The intercom system is a clunky, generic box wedged in a rough hole in the hallway wall. A silver speaker, a lone red button, pubic curls of wire erupting. Shaker studies the fickle appliance. "That's a whole lot of fire hazard for one dinky box."

"Tons of fringe benefits at that pet store," Darb says. "When the old technology conks out, it's up for grabs. Lorelei snatched this beauty from the animal grooming snobs. I installed it myself. Nice, eh?"

Darb thumbs the buzzer.

"Mort? Mortimer?" He unclicks the button, thinks a moment, clicks it again. "Liberteen?"

Darb shifts around on his feet, neck cords rising, pinkness smearing his forehead. A long pause. Then he rears back and hollers at the door, "I am no longer declaring myself with this stupid box!"

The intercom crackles and a helium voice replies, "I'm down here."

"I know you're *down there*, damn it! Come upstairs! Enjoy some supper with your progenitor and his kin. We can eat the last of that seaweed sushi platter. Meet us out back on the launch pad."

"Liberteen?" Shaker asks his cousin.

Darb gives an impatient tap with his foot. "Let's go look at the trampoline again."

The backyard is strewn with faded oak carcasses. The slim margin of grass that surrounds Darb's numerous efforts of unfinished husbandry has been leeched of its color. The cousins stand amid this pared landscape, sifting their words with titanic care.

"I'm not gonna ask about a paternity test," says Shaker.

"Good," replies Darb. "One day we'll see how much like me he grows up to be."

"We can only hope he holds onto more of his hair."

"I *got* my hair!"

"It's doing that rimming thing."

"Least I got a house. A whole one."

"You share it with people."

"*My* people," Darb grins fiercely. "Don't erode me, cousin."

He's holding so much oxygen in his lungs, maintaining the grin, that his face reddens, his skin huge with veiny corrugations. The marble-swirled buttons on his sweater vest are ready to pop off. Shaker takes a step back, turns, and points.

"There is a strange man in gym pants watching us from your kitchen."

"That's him," Darb says.

"Your son?"

"Try to avoid looking him straight in the eye," Darb whispers as the kid comes clodding out the sliding door. He is a colossal-sized young man, neckless and chinless, with ineptly cropped hair and the palest skin Shaker has ever seen outside the municipal zoo. The boy plods nearer, tugging at his mesh athletic jersey, looking only at the ground. Then when he stands adjacent from Darb, his head swings high, too high, and the teenager's dead stare reorients to his father's shrinking hairline.

"I sure do love counting the follicles up in your nostrils," Darb tells him. "Say hi to Uncle Shaker."

"I'm reading about tetrodotoxin."

"Wonderful," Darb replies. "Tell the gentleman hi."

"You go shopping?" asks the helium voice.

"Say hi first."

"Hi first. You go shopping yet?"

"Hell, who needs hair when I got this young stud!"

Darb hugs his son so hard he almost squeezes the very DNA out of him. The kid whimpers and cringes. Shrill avian decibels escape from his throat.

Darb is doing the rapid arm-paddle again.

"Hey sorry," he stammers. "I forgot, no touchies. Fish food's with mom. Enter the garage at your own risk."

Mortimer nods anxiously, brushes his bad haircut into a mannered part and immediately demolishes it, then fixes a direct stare on Shaker's left eyebrow, which maybe—Shaker admits—could use some aggressive tweezing.

The boy concludes his visit with an impish cluck of his tongue and flees back into the house. Shaker ponders the backyard for a long while, rubbing his cheek stubble's elusive grain.

"Tetra-what?" he asks.

"No idea," Darb sighs, then looks up chipperly. "Wanna check out the intercom again?"

*

Darb offers to drive him, but Shaker opts to walk home alone. The autumn air feels loose and unsullied and convinces Shaker he may someday stride headlong through this mud- and snot-glutted world without having to first borrow someone else's galoshes. In the interim, he tries not to walk too jagged a line. He had been a broad, hulking youth himself, mostly forehead and knuckle, with mangy hair before it was in vogue and a disconcerting smoker's rasp although he did not smoke. He roamed the halls of his high school in a cruddy denim jacket faded with acid wash, and he bullied for small change but always bashfully, which made the larceny seem almost charitable. Whenever he skulked around the cafeteria or school assemblies, he had a habit of whipping his head sideward, trying to keep the hair out of his field of vision, which was already impaired, kudos his inhalant intake of the period. His complexion was sympathetically referred to as "rough." An estranged teenager, but amiable, floundering in his own nervous juices. His sneakers were always a little too large and a little too white.

And now? He feels like an ancient coral rock or mollusk marooned on a sunburnt beach after some great tide has receded. The beach is Doris's doorstep. Shaker pauses at the top of the stairs, trying to remember the secret knock, when the door swings open.

Doris is winterized in a snowflake kimono and flannel pj's and cold-creamed face. She looks blazed clean, ready for bed. Shaker isn't sure how he looks, although he knows his hair is unwashed and his lung cavity is scarred black with smoked fish guts. He nods at Doris and peers around her into the house. Several half-clothed men are seated in a circle on the floor with clothespins attached to their extremities. They are united by the ropey tentacles of a hookah apparatus. A racy powwow of some sort.

"I see you're holding court," Shaker says. "Room for one more?"

"Oh, you don't want to mingle with this crowd, Shaker. You're too much a gentleman."

"Those fellas."

"Yes?"

"Their genitals are clothes-pinned."

"I hadn't noticed," she smiles.

"You're the only one who thinks I'm a gentleman."

"Oh, I don't really think that, dear. I don't think that *at all*. But I like the way your expression goes haywire whenever I say it."

"I found Darb."

"I didn't know he was missing."

"He was," Shaker says. "I brought him all the way back from Tuscaloosa for you."

"Well, I don't want the diseased trash. I don't even know where Tuscaloosa is!"

Shaker rubs the middle of his chest, the hard sternum, the dead fish.

"The other side of the earth," he tells her.

8.

The supermarket aisles have a heavenly veneer that prevents Shaker from feeling too embarrassed about the ensemble. The suit is secondhand, a thrift-shop special, cornflower blue. His hair has been greased into a sharp pompadour already starting to avalanche on one side. He admires his reflection in the high freezer doors and smooths the pressed creases of each pant leg, touches up the isosceles hairdo, and moves onward around the meat bins and poultry racks. In the next aisle, a stock boy is lining and leveling a shelf of celebrity-endorsed sour creams. He offers Shaker a friendly salutation. Shaker responds with a careful bow of his gelled head. Then he opens his wallet and gives the young man a coupon redeemable for one free vanilla milkshake at General Custard's Last Stand. The young man squints curiously, trying to distinguish Shaker in all the manufactured brightness. Shaker has already moved on down the aisle, a swing in each step, feeling like a joyously brain-damaged Fred Astaire.

*

But nobody answers when he knocks. Shaker juggles the package to his other arm and tries the doorbell. The house is half-lit, the rear half, the half he can't quite see. So Shaker gives the screen door a peevish kick, and when that doesn't rouse anything he goes to the garage, where he's able to discern the woman folded into an origami knot on her yoga mat. The garage is locked. Shaker waits for eye contact. He tries to tell himself there is nothing arousing at all about the knuckled shape of a female in spandex. He puts his warm forehead against the cold pane and pounds the pair of alien surfaces together until Lorelei rises, a skinny stalk in tights, and rolls open the garage door.

"I can stand here all day," Shaker says.

The woman smiles her pretty, blank smile and uncorks an earplug.

"Good afternoon," Shaker says, the middle of evening.

Her smile remains. The blankness, too.

"Dinner," he says. He holds up the prepackaged chicken breast, vacuum-suctioned to a Styrofoam slab.

"I don't know when he'll be back," she replies.

"He's somewhere else tonight?"

"It's already been a week."

"A week."

Shaker gazes at her serene and healthy face, a smile that could not be taken off with a claw hammer or shovel. A single BB of sweat is slugging down her sleek neck.

"Those tights really are something," Shaker mumbles.

Lorelei absently brushes at the sweaty bangs pinned above her hairline. The barrettes are plastic butterflies, colorful, a child's. She pinches a piece of spandex, stretches and snaps it, and she leads him into the house.

The kitchen with its cream walls and Japanese tapestries appears not to have been used since Shaker's last visit. The cupboard holds three plates, three bowls, three tureens. Lorelei points at the mat on the floor, and Shaker sets it with a couple utensils and cloth napkins. He's examining the series of complicated oven dials with a sense of subtle yet encroaching horror when she makes her move for the garage.

"I don't even like poultry," he blurts.

Lorelei halts in the doorway, regarding him with that intense and empty smile. Shaker's mouth muscles are weary, so weary, of trying to match it. The chicken meal has been set on the floor. Now Shaker nudges it with a scuffed loafer.

"You are a funny one," she says and slips out the door.

Shaker ambles into the den. There is only blank wall to occupy him. He leans over the couch and sees that Darb's rump indentations are circled in red paint, a large bull's-eye stained on the cushion. Shaker sniffs the industrial acrylic and recognizes the brand. Then he sniffs some more—extravagant, lungy whiffs—and he stares at the hypnotic design until his vision wobbles and he must leave the room.

The intercom in the hall with its slack wires and shoddy encasement is no closer to completion. Shaker shores himself up in his silly little suit and opens the basement door. The boy meets him halfway up the staircase. At least Shaker presumes this is the boy. Mort. Mortimer. Liberteen. The big-boned savant is concealed inside a polyester tracksuit and a gasmask inherited from the halcyon days of international trench warfare.

"Gas leak?" Shaker asks.

He lifts his shirt collar over his nose, train-robber style, and puts out his hand, which the boy refuses to take.

"Looks like you're my dinner date," Shaker says in a muffled voice.

The boy moves with such assured dispatch Shaker thinks dreamily of endangered pachyderms and their startled stampede. It's almost majestic, that kind of panic in concentrate. He follows the large, nimble-footed adolescent into the kitchen, watching the back of the boy's head and the mask straps that mush his neck pork, his surly cowlicks.

Shaker and the boy sit on the linoleum like meditating swamis and wait for their chicken to cook in the oven.

"You're going to wear that mask throughout our meal, aren't you?" Shaker says.

The gasmask gives him a slow nod.

"Very hip," Shaker replies.

Shaker is distractedly toying with a utensil, drumming his kneecaps, batting his earlobe. Even behind the murky lenses, he can sense the boy's steadfast stare, mental machinery slamming back and forth like an antique loom.

Shaker puts down the spoon and unshirts his mouth.

"Your mother seems exceptionally limber," he says. "Do you have a real father somewhere?"

The lenses only glare back.

Shaker fetches the chicken wedges, plates them, and he and the boy spend the rest of the dinner hour staring hungerlessly at their plates, not touching a thing. Eventually, Shaker points at the sliding glass door.

"Any objections?" he asks.

They step outside among the range of unfinished projects that mar the backyard.

Shaker shakes his head.

"I can't do any better than that," he says.

*

But the following day he's back, standing on the same spot in his civilian duds. Lorelei is away at work, and Darb's still gone. Shaker listens to Mortimer stir around the basement all afternoon, the teenager occasionally venturing upstairs to commandeer some knickknack or appliance, still wearing the same tracksuit, the gasmask. He ignores Shaker completely, much to Shaker's relief. Shaker is more interested in the intercom in its sloppy hole. One summer in high school, he toiled part-time as an electrician's assistant's assistant, switching out light bulbs, re-ballasting fixtures and exit signs, and sweeping up the accidental breakage, flagrant amounts of it. Now he studies the intercom's exposed guts and decides the wiring should be replaced.

So Shaker lures the boy into the truck by promising him a greasy, artery-stuffing, fast-food meal at the end of their trip, and together they drive to Softy's Hardware Warehouse, where they wander the aisles like beleaguered trick-or-treaters, piling a basket with random supplies: brackets, lug nuts, cable, solder, anything Shaker might involve in his experimental operation. They fill the basket and start a second.

"Building an ark," he tells the old man at the register.

"Say again?" Old Softy is square-built, his hips broad as his shoulders, all neck wattle and gland. And mostly deaf.

"An ark!" Shaker shouts into his hairy ear. "Two of them!"

Softy comes alive a little and giggles. "We're having a sale on sump-pumps. In case of flood."

"That so."

"Not really."

"I'll take twenty-five," Shaker says with a wink.

The ride back to Darb's house, however, Shaker can't stop winking. His whole head is overtaken by this aberrant spasm. His vision flickers, the eyelid aches. He swats himself on the cheekbone repeatedly, and this only makes the eye flinch faster.

Shaker is forced to pull off the road.

"My head is broken," he whispers. "God is trying to humiliate me."

Mortimer remains calm in his seat, staring impassively at the road and the early cold front that is unsettling so many birds from the trees. The birds rise in clusters, like foliage shedding in reverse. This adds one more melancholy item to Shaker's growing roster. The boy straightens the gasmask on his face, pulls Shaker into the passenger seat, and drives the rest of the way home with a confidence and precision that even Shaker, half-blind, can see.

Perhaps it's the soothing drive that restores his muscle control. Shaker stands in the hallway, blinkless and relaxed, with the hot solder gun in his hand and the smoke of newly sutured wire stimulating his nostrils. The box, the extra brackets, a plastic telephone mouthpiece, fresh wiring, all melded into a rather handsome package. Shaker tries the button. It doesn't work. He fiddles and tries again. Nothing.

He shrugs and says, "Olé," but the boy has already returned to the basement. The lug nuts and excess length of solder wire have apparently gone there with him.

Outdoors, the cold front relents. The sun hangs on the horizon like an irritated boil. It burns a bit brighter than usual, but maybe that's just the sweat in Shaker's eyes.

*

Later that evening, Shaker is back at Darb's house with a six-pack of generic near-beer and an amorphous glow in his chest. He goes down to the basement. The room is mostly stacked boxes and blanketed shapes, and Shaker is forced to stoop to avoid thudding his head on the drop ceiling. He follows the sound of squishing liquids and an electric hum to Mortimer's workbench in the far corner.

The wall above the bench is a pastiche of scientific doodles and schematics, pages torn from high school chemistry books, Boy Scout badges. Daisy-chained around the area on the floor and shelves is an abundant clutter of apparatus. Rubber tubing, foils, funnels, sieves and saucepans, kitty litter, multiple hot plates plugged into the same power strip, fish food, and an enormous wall-length aquarium of neon puffers. Dozens and dozens. Some are shingled, some spotted, striated. Shaker stands on the cusp, hydrating with one near-beer after the other, as Mortimer crushes a seedy powder with mortar and pestle. Beside the bench, twentysome boxes originally labeled *PUFFER*, but the word has been X'd out and replaced with *BLOWFISH*.

"You need any help with quality control? A lab rat? Guinea pig? Any free samples?" But the kid ignores him.

Shaker snatches an egg timer from the clutter and bobbles it in his beerless hand. He watches the boy, faintly and bewildered, the ticking device clutched against his chest like a second, smarter heart.

*

That night, Shaker drifts into a rambling route home. He's putting so many miles on the Tully truck he feels obligated to wash it in the morning, refill some fluids, maybe give it a new coat of paint. Instead, he will slash its quartet of tires and leave the vehicle abandoned in a shady grove seven miles from the Tully house. That just feels like the right thing, the most Shaker thing, to do. Now he drives with the windows open and the air pushing in. He tries to take a dirt road that sidewinds up a small ridge, his secret shortcut, but he gets lost and has to backtrack. The night is starless but warm. He keeps giving the truck's radio dirty looks.

When he enters his duplex he toggles the light switch, but the room remains dark. Shaker stumbles forward. He reaches for the lamp cord, but he can't find the cord, or the lamp, or the table where the lamp is supposed to be located. Shaker rummages blindly around the kitchen for some candles or a flashlight and finds the drawers are empty. The only source of illumination is the single bulb on the Hoosters' half of the back porch. Shaker props himself against the wall, arms folded, testily waiting for his eyesight to adjust. The rooms brighten, but nothing materializes. The futon mattress and wood frame, key rack, radio, dead plant, foldable chairs, the rug and card table and lamp, and the magazine pages he glued to the wall in a sorry-assed attempt at bachelor décor. Everything is gone. The duplex is as empty as the day he moved in. Emptier, even.

Shaker walks onto the patio and sees the beach chair now sits on the Hooster side. Looks cleaner, brighter, installed in a happier life. He nods with new understanding and raps on the girl's window.

"I know," the girl sighs. "I saw the moving truck."

"A whole truck?"

"More like a station wagon."

Shaker tries not to look so deflated.

"I see you got the chair," he says.

"He said I had to ask you."

"Thanks for rooting against the home team."

"The muscles on that dude!"

"Yes," Shaker says. "You're just a teen. The oyster is your world."

"So can I keep it? The guy left a phone number to call."

"Teléfono, por favor." He holds out a hand.

The Hooster girl gathers up the excess cord and stretches the phone out the window to Shaker, who is unexpectedly flustered at the courtesy.

"Thanks," he says shyly and digs a few grubby cents from his pocket and slaps them on the sill. "For the concierge."

The girl reaches through the window and touches a finger to Shaker's temple.

"Think that guy stole more than your crummy house," the girl says.

"Enjoy the chair," Shaker replies, reading the number written in sharpie on her arm. He dials it so quick he doesn't have time to parse the half-baked schemes and cookie crumbs and sheep manure that currently clog his mental chute.

"Take it all," he says as soon as someone picks up. "The glass in the windows, the silver fillings in my teeth. It's all yours. Everything."

Shaker hears only heavy breath, the scratching of facial hair. What Shaker imagines to be a sinister goatee.

"It's okay," Shaker continues. "That futon was giving me rashes. I didn't really fit on it. I forgive you, whoever you are."

The scratching halts. A slow hiss of silence.

"You haven't atoned for your sins," the voice says.

"I didn't know I had any."

"That's not our problem."

"So how do I atone?"

"You can't."

Shaker pauses. "I still forgive you, guy."

"So you think this is how you whup us?" the voice asks. "Turn the other cheek? Give us the Gandhi? Shame us?"

"Maybe."

"You fucker," the man says and hangs up.

Shaker is still holding the phone to his head like a conch shell he has unburied at the beach, unable to decide if the bogus ocean sounds warrant a spot on the bookshelf or not. There is no more bookshelf, Shaker reminds himself, and he relays the phone to the Hooster girl, who has watched the entire exchange while keeping one eye on a portable TV. The dark room strobes with each fresh image. She unmutes the volume and regards Shaker as if he has an ugly clot of vegetable lodged between his incisors.

"You are a mess," the girl tells him.

"Thank you."

"Mama thinks you'd be an item if you got a real wardrobe and didn't sustain all those mongrels with milk like an old spinster. And by 'wardrobe' I don't think she means that dumpy outfit you were wearing a few days ago."

"Listen," Shaker says, clinging on her windowsill. "Can you—"

"I ain't lending my bike for you to break again."

"It's not the bike I want to borrow."

"Then what?"

Shaker reaches through the window and rubs an uneven splotch of acne cream across the rest of the girl's nose.

"How do you feel about trench warfare?"

*

Shaker is wearing his part of the bargain, an oversized seersucker thing the girl selected from the thrift-shop rack: three pieces, pinstriped, an ascot knotted at the neck. Shaker feels like he is dressed for a high school musical set during the dark days of Prohibition. He avoids the dandyish sight of himself in the restaurant mirror and continues to scrutinize the dinner menu even after their ravioli has arrived. The Hooster woman will not stop rubbing the ribbed fabric on Shaker's arm. He looks for the waiter to order more ice water, buckets of it, tankers, and he accidentally catches the Hooster woman's eye.

"I hear everything on the other side of our living room wall," she says. "Does that upset you?"

"We could have had lasagna," he mutters.

"You are a lonely man."

"Cod fish. Chicken parm."

"And you're afraid of lonely women. You're *terrified* of us. You think we're going to come charging over the hilltop in a big posse with pitchforks and prenuptial agreements."

"Uh oh," he says, sniffing his spoon and looking up. "Does this ravioli have eggplant in it? I can't be anywhere near eggplant."

"I can hear your drunk weeping at night, those sad songs you try to sing. Even your bathroom noises. It's disgusting. God knows what you hear of us."

"A lot of vacuuming," Shaker says.

"We don't own a vacuum."

"I know," he nods. "That's what horrifies me."

The Hooster woman leans across the table and whispers, "I used to be afraid like you. You know what I realized? The unbeatable slow machine that chews up your life? That machine is scared, too. So I made a little investment to even things up. Would you like to see my cannon?"

She's holding Shaker at the wrist now. Both wrists.

"God no," he says.

"You're gun-shy."

"I don't own a vacuum, either."

The Hooster woman releases Shaker's arms and fixes her posture, straight and serious, and looks around the room. She points a fake fingernail tip at the sternest, most behemoth-scale man at the restaurant bar.

"That ox," she says. "Could you fight him?"

"Why would I fight him?"

"To defend my honor."

"Your honor is fine, just fine."

"Prove it."

"I'd rather not," Shaker says.

The Hooster woman smiles hard and starched, the way Shaker imagines cosmopolitan ladies regard each other in line at the lingerie store. She swallows a few spoonfuls of her ravioli, wipes her mouth, raises an arm, and motions for the muscled man.

"Hey, ox!" she shouts.

When Shaker recovers from the blackout, he is in the backseat of the woman's automobile, his ascot vanished, his seersucker awry. The Hooster woman is nestled against him with a pearl-handled revolver in her lap.

"That wasn't so bad, was it?" she says.

Shaker taps the raw lump on his cheek. That is either blood or ravioli sauce slathered all over him and the gun.

"Did you pistol-smack me?" he asks.

"Somebody had to shoehorn some manhood into you. Mr. Ox was much too nice. Do you think the gun is loaded? The machine doesn't *sleep*."

Shaker cannot nod without aggravating his migraine, no matter how much he agrees with her. He groans a humble affirmation. He feels around the seat for a take-out carton or doggy bag. The Hooster woman sits up, kisses his injury, then licks the gun barrel and touches it to the doughy spot on his person where he maybe still has a liver or spleen.

"Bang bang," she whispers.

*

The next morning, Shaker wakes to a sprained face, vaguely regretful the woman is not humped on him in his borrowed sleeping bag, hair snarled wild, cooing gun puns. He slouches around the duplex until noon, and then he makes the long foot-trek to Tullys for their truck. The Brothers are so inured to this scene they don't bother to stir from their tree post in the side yard. Tully One waves hello with his rifle snout while Brother Two goes for the notepad, adding a checkmark to the continuing tally. Neither Tully mentions the tires Shaker slashed, the rearview mirror he busted. Shaker is running out of surfaces to paint. Soon the entire house will be a runny seafoam green, and they'll be asking him to sand off the color and start anew. Maybe a loud chartreuse. Eggplant purple. Black-eye black.

"She broke me in alright," Shaker later tells the Hooster girl, who nods grimly at his new shiner. "Probably needs x-rays."

"Does this halter make me look slutty?"

She thrusts the fuchsia top through the window and into Shaker's face. Instinctively, he flinches.

"It's fine," he says. "Perfectly respectable."

"Then I don't want it on me."

He can hear her rummaging in congested bureaus, kicking aside wire hangers, burrowing into boxes. Shut-eyed again, he reaches in an arm and drags out the alarm clock by its cord.

"It's almost five."

"So?" she asks.

"Best to catch him before suppertime, when his appetite is starting to crest."

"Whoever heard about a goddamn date to Burger World?"

"He likes his fast food."

"And you'll wait in the car?"

Shaker shakes his head. "I'll hang back at the house. Play with his fish."

"Sounds like a real hot time," she sighs.

"Deal's a deal," Shaker says, ducking at the sound of her mother's voice in heated communion with a talk radio program in the next room. When he rises again, the girl is standing in knee-high socks and bicycle shorts and a t-shirt fringed with large rips.

"It looks like somebody tossed you to the lions."

"Don't I know it," the girl replies.

They drive with the windows unrolled, a tide of air moving through the truck. The stereo is off, but the girl is perusing the collection of bootlegs—all Shaker's ex-wife—that reappeared in the backseat. The girl hums a half-forgotten song. Her pitch is unsteady, a brief warble concluding her high notes. Shaker himself is tone deaf, music deaf. He could not establish a stable rhythm with a metronome wired to his cochlea. The girl's fluted sounds make him uneasy.

"You mind not doing that?" he asks.

"I'm that bad? My voice?"

"Nah. Maybe. I dunno."

"You're the gruesome one."

Shaker nods, tapping at the wheel with erratic canter. "I just want to be the type who brings his own galoshes."

"You smell like unshowered rutabaga, too."

The truck is halfway to Darb's when the girl begins to scoot in her seat, heels knocking, anxiously winding her fingers in shirt fringe.

"Nervous?" he asks.

"See that gas station?" she says. The building is abandoned, decrepit. "I'm gonna pee myself if we don't stop."

"Land ho," Shaker replies and slows the truck into the pebbled lot. Two rusted pumps, a snack shack that has been shuttered, an ice machine in manacles. Shaker conducts a speedy reconnaissance and stands guard between the truck and the girl as she disappears around the shack's corner. Road traffic is sporadic. Shaker waits with his head at a gallant tilt, chin high, arms crossed, arms uncrossed. He's not really sure what to do with his arms. A car passes, another. Shaker waves. He gets a few smiles in response, a few unpleasant gestures. He waves again and again, working his arm in exaggerated arcs, like a political novice campaigning for a municipal post that has not been adequately described to him. Once the routine turns stale, he walks back to the truck, where the Hooster girl is sitting and watching him, big-eyed, baffled. Shaker waves at one last station wagon as it goes streaking by.

"Mama wasn't lying. You are an odd egg."

"And my gum lines are receding," he nods.

The girl fires up the cassette player, and Shaker allows it. The unmistakable voice of his ex-wife ambushes him in stereophonic sound. The recording is rough, muddy, a series of subdued declarations taking place in an oak-echoed room. Some kind of legal deposition. Shaker dials down the volume but lets the tape spool through the stereo while the girl resumes humming in her slatternly getup, and they drive.

It's almost six. Suppertime soon. They are approaching the last bend of road. Something charred and tangy enters their nostrils. Shaker and the girl smell the inferno before they see it. Darb's house. It has been replaced by a holocaust of orange flame.

"Is that?" she asks. "Is it?"

The disaster area is tended by fire trucks and ambulances and a corps of plainclothes policemen and lifeguards in neon rain-slickers who holler into their walkie-talkies and conduct traffic farther down the road. Shaker settles the truck into a rocky ditch but cannot climb out. Instead, he watches the scene slivered in the rearview mirror, the girl beside him wan, silent. He sees a fireman dislodge himself from his helmet and proceed to drench hair and head in the full force of a pressurized hose. Other workers prod the ground with pickaxes and tamp debris. There is an authentic Dalmatian dog inside the fire truck, slobbering the glass in expressionistic swirls. A male cop, grease-smeared, yawning, massages the shoulders of a female EMT. And the smoke. The dark smoke rises, infinite in measure, pulled and pulled and pulled from the inferno, remaking the sky in a not-unbeautiful slate.

"Stay here," Shaker croaks and tugs his arm free, unaware the girl has been squeezing his hand. To his surprise, nobody stops him. He does an awkward limbo under the caution tape and approaches an ambulance, steeling himself for the horror, any horror, shrouded or toe-tagged or unsheeted or slabbed. Lorelei sits on a stretcher, pristine in her leotard spandex, an oxygen mask clamped against her mouth. Beside her, an EMT is in distracted consultation with a clipboard. The young man peppers her with curt questions and nods and nods and unstraps the inflatable band from her bicep. Shaker can't hear much. He's too numb for sound. The smell is a putrid garbage rot, the kind of thing that makes retching feel like pure, dry relief. Then Shaker is knocked away by a pair of workers transporting a collapsible table, which they erect at the caution-tape cordon and adorn with disposable cups, a coffee carafe, plates of pastries. The Dalmatian is barking for its dinner now. A rescue worker slots his ax in a melted lump of stucco and heads for the truck, crooning with puppy yammer, unable to allay the animal. Shaker pushes through the mass of men who have flocked around the coffee table. He finds Darb sitting on the fender of a police cruiser, a blanket on one leg, his son's gasmask clutched in his hands.

"This was all I could get," Darb says, strangling the rubber mask, his own face smeared with cinder, damp grief. "The rest of him was melted to the workbench."

There are third-degree burns up his arms and wrists, flesh in blister, his tropical-theme shirt nightmarishly singed, the little that's left of it. His socks are blackened to his feet. It's here Shaker notices the team of EMTs in a semi-circle around the car and Darb. The EMTs are overloaded with splints and gauzes and compresses, a neck brace that seems on loan from another catastrophe entirely. They're waiting for Shaker's cousin to submit to treatment. Darb, unable to meet Shaker's gaze, regards them all with bitter contempt. Shaker doesn't try to formulate any kind of speech, let alone condolence. He simply wriggles off his seersucker vest, eases forward, and tenderly smacks the smolder from Darb's charred half-shirt. When he steps back, the EMTs move in. Darb looks at Shaker now, unblinkingly, an agonized stare. Shaker wants to say something, any dumb something. But his attention shifts as one of the EMTs produces a scorched piece of tubing he has rescued from the wreckage. There are rigorous nods, condescending sniffs. The man smirks at Darb and grumbles the words "drug-cook flambé."

And then Darb is restored to his feet and has the man's throat between his hands. The EMTs pile on, six or seven of them, each restraining a different Darb limb, doubling-up on his flailing arms. He's cracking jaws and headbutting blindly, one hand still pressing down on the smirker's neck. Then the cops enter the rumble, a few swaggering firemen. The EMT emerges from the brawl kneading his own throat. He sits on a bumper and pops an antacid pill, fitting himself into the unused neck brace.

Shaker and the girl stay until Darb is handcuffed and escorted off the premises in an unmarked vehicle, and it is already the next morning. Lorelei's ambulance left hours ago. The ruins are sending up smoke signals en masse, a swizzle of gray-black messages that all say the same dark thing. The cop cruisers scatter in different directions. The firemen depart with their slumbering Dalmation, and Shaker and the Hooster girl stand beside the empty buffet table, the snacks eaten, the carafe drained. Only the gasmask, found on the ground and tossed against the bagel spread as an afterthought, remains.

Then they go.

*

The sun peeks over the hillside. They are driving home at a fraction of the speed limit. Shaker knows that if the girl attended school on a regular basis, she would be readying for the bus at this hour. She'd be gobbling breakfast with her hair in an electric straightener, her homework unfinished, or sassing her mother, or telling her mother she loved her, or reminding herself at least she had a mother to love. Or maybe she'd just sit there, staring down and softly cursing her oily skin and angular hips. The girl is dozing in the passenger seat instead, curled into herself for warmth, the seersucker shading her face. Shaker steers but doesn't see the road. All is weightless and light. He is coherent enough to understand there are gradations to shock, cloverleaf ramps, loading docks, staging areas. But none of that interests him. The road is gone. The wheel fills his grip. He wants to navigate the truck to the nearest rest stop and rescue a litter of emaciated puppies from a flash flood or forest blaze. He wants to hold high the leaky roof of heaven and provide shelter to all the premature widows and abandoned orphans who do not have enough ceiling in their lives. He wants to do any number of pointless, impossible things.

They arrive home to half a house. Shaker's side has vanished. Just the shared wall and its ugly lime paint are standing. Each of his rooms has been thoroughly bulldozed, the debris and dirt carted off, plumbing pipes and electrical wiring sucked back into the soil, and neatly. The remaining hardwood floor is blackened with an earthmover's tread, naked to the elements. Shaker feels like all the near and far cataclysms in his life are aligning, end to end, a spooky eclipse. And maybe he feels some reassurance in this.

The Hooster girl is awake and coolly gazing out the windshield, also unimpressed.

"You said they could take it all," she says.

"I did."

"House sorta looks bigger now in a weird way."

"You're right," Shaker says, filling with a terrible awe. "It does."

"If Mama asks—"

"I'll explain."

"Don't," she says. "Just tell her I ran off like usual and it took you all night to find me. I'll only be grounded a week."

"But—"

"I gotta go wash my hair," she says. "It's the only thing I can smell."

She leans up and pecks Shaker on the cheek and wears his coat pulled around her waist as she carefully swings her skinny legs out the truck and across the bare tract. Most of the property is now patio. Shaker gets out of the truck as well, taking a few short strides and promptly lying down in the churned earth. There is no tingle in his reconstructed knee; the pins and rods are quiet. His head is hollow, immaculate. Shaker imagines picking up one of those starved puppies he has rescued and snuggling it against his crusted mouth and vacant forehead, then squeezing the small animal as its adorable eyes go big and dreadful and the squirming dog explodes like a jelly donut. Then he imagines exploding another and another and another and another until the entire world has been reduced to Shaker, his bloody hands, and an empty cardboard box.

Thus at long last, exhausted by all that imaginary puppy slaughter, Shaker can shut his eyes, and it suddenly seems like an alright idea to have a loud, ferocious crying jag right there on his peaceful yard.

PART TWO

9.

Shaker rolls belly up in the sunlight. He can visualize the narrow range, one yard to another yard, his purview. He plumbs his mouth with a knuckle. He takes his air in meek lungfuls, like a beached goldfish gasping through a mouth-hole too small for its face. This face is not much in aggregate. Very little percolates under it. Conversely, a fleet of miniature aircraft continues to wheel several miles overhead. Their contrails are daubed across the sky's concavity and beyond, reminding Shaker of his favorite brand of commercial toothpaste.

Let go my purview, he thinks.

He doesn't notice the Hooster woman until she scoops his head into her lap. She tilts him backwards, reaches into her zebra-print bathrobe, and produces a thermos. The monochrome construction-worker kind. The thermos cap is affixed with an absurdly long crazy straw. She stabs the novelty item into Shaker's mouth with a great deal of relish. Shaker sips the apricot swill and blinks his approval. The Hooster woman cradles him tenderly, picking the mulch and dried tear dew from his cheek.

The mongrel dogs that besieged his home are gone. The home is gone. The Hooster woman kisses his brow and returns him to his moldering spot on the ground. There is some kind of sofa sham underneath him, a homemade needlepoint. It is stitched with Day of the Dead sugar skulls, perky and bejeweled. Shaker closes his eyes and listens to the sound of the woman's slippers padding away across the grass. The door to the former duplex shuts. Shaker is alone with the dirt and the mulch and the dark business of his own body. He can feel his heartbeat all the way up in his armpit. The gaps between his ribs are filled with toe jam. Blood spurt, muscle hum, an idiot drone. His interior currents won't abate.

Shaker cannot remember the last time he utilized a straw that didn't somehow end up a nostril.

*

Breakfast is wheat toast saturated with cream cheese and jelly and a side of scrambled brains. This morning's negligee is patterned in cheetah. The Hooster woman really layers on the perfume, a debutante fragrance with floral accents to which Shaker has grown addicted, sniffing at the aroma she left in the yard. He licks his dishes and cutlery spotless and dries them with his shirt. All her fine china is arrayed tidily in the grass. He regulates his breathing to a steady bombast. He tells himself if he ever rises and returns to civilization, he will purchase this woman a modest outdoor patio set.

Lunch, however, does not come. And when dinner isn't delivered, Shaker begins to worry he has broken decorum in some significant fashion. Maybe he was supposed to return the silverware by pitching it underhand into one of her open windows. Maybe he should have flashed around that dimwit smile of his, or said please and thank you, or vetted the newspapers that are amassing atop him in the yard. Shaker has slipped into too many kinds of flux. The flux is the only interesting thing about him. Shaker sits up and enjoys the tilt of purview. From this vantage, it's much easier to hear the impatient throat-clearing behind him. Shaker crabwalks a half-circle. The Hooster woman is lit diagonal by porch lamp, a Rorschach blend of panda prints and lacy underthings, bare leg thrust out.

"Well?" she says. "Are we gonna pity-fuck the sadness out of each other or what?"

Shaker shakes the muddled blood from his brain, fixes his hair, and follows her to bed.

*

The Hooster woman's bedroom is a mirror image of Shaker's old abode. Same marled plaster ceiling and layout and dimensions, only backwards and stained with nicotine colors and smells, drizzle leak. Shaker barely notices the uncanniness of it. The sex is not surprising, either. The dirty flirters, Shaker has found, are usually the most missionary partners. They exhaust themselves on eighty different ways of uttering "mount me" until there's nothing left to do but lay stiff-spraddled and ride out the long fuck. The long fuck is actually quite agreeable. Shaker is also partial to the woman's post-coital coos, even if they are babbled in her sleep. He gives her a deep nuzzle and licks an earlobe. She coos more loudly, and he kisses her neck. Then he carefully pries the blanket from underneath her snoring body, capes himself with it, and returns to the yard.

*

When the rainfall finds him, it arrives sideways and in syncopated bursts spritzing him in the face, so he belly-worms over to a dry swatch of grass where the yard sprinklers cannot harass him. A note, he realizes, is pinned to his shoe. Shaker looks back at the half-house, the road, but the messenger has disappeared. The sprinkler water has blurred much of the note's contents. Shaker wrings out the sodden sheet, flattens it, holds it up to the sunlight, and squints.

Sorry about the house, chief. Just doing my job. I tried not to damage the landscaping too much, but you of all people must appreciate how unwieldy large lawn machinery can be. My employers are really satisfied with the project. There's a group of them, a kind of committee. I realize now you don't remember what you did to deserve all of this. Too late to worry about it, I guess. If it's any consolation, they're all pretty nice folks, and they pay well. If you're ever looking for a little work...

Shaker balls up the note and eats it for a noontime snack.

*

Shaker's torpor is interrupted only by the mailman and local children at play, garrulous dog-walkers dragged along by their yipping, leashed packs. He also has a fuzzy recollection of an unknown pedestrian trying to scalp him with an ice scraper, but maybe that was a fever dream. Shaker suspects the attack would have been totally justified, although he'd rather not investigate the exact source of his remorse. He just knows the remorse is stashed away in a mungy pit far inside him, accruing interest slowly—moss and lice, too—for review at some future date.

And now the Tullys. Both Brothers are costumed in one-piece hazmat suits, the type worn by waste-handlers, bomb squads, asbestos removal teams. Their faceplates are smogged over, their respiration labored. The Tullys crouch near him. Shaker winces upon seeing the haggard man, sunburned and bum-bearded, reflected in their helmeted heads. All that's missing from the vision are catheters twisting out his every dim hole, a colostomy pouch.

Tully One seems ready to speak, but Shaker immediately interrupts.

"Please, no talk," he pleads raspily. "That's the shtick. If you don't break shtick, you get to keep your catheters in place."

Shaker raises his hands to count.

"Twenty days I had that truck. Figure eight hours' labor a day. Factor in the late fee, the service surcharge, the sales tax, the black-market payola. Maybe I dig you guys an in-ground pool or construct a tornado shelter out of popsicle sticks."

The second Tully has taken a newspaper from the yard and knocks it apart for Shaker to read. The fallout has made the front page. Darb is estimated to get six months in the clink for throttling the first responder. Lorelei has already been remanded into the custody of Tuscaloosa authorities on several outstanding warrants, most involving identity theft. Shaker hypothesizes she will go on to be reformed and resocialized and perish in a poignant act of self-immolation via gasoline-soaked yoga spandex or tofu poisoning. And the boy, the poor boy. Local media have vilified him variously as a precocious drug-ring mastermind, bumpkin trash, a klutz, although no one can agree what drug he manufactured. Shaker doesn't even know if there was enough of the boy left to bury. No mention is made of the origin of the blaze, i.e., if it involved a poorly re-repaired intercom system or not.

"Probably not my fault," he says, ignoring the sick pinch in his stomach, and he waves away the paper.

The first Tully has taped a new sign to the truck's flank. TULLY BROTHERS REMAINDERING AND WRECKAGE REMOVAL. EVICTIONS. DOMESTIC CATASTROPHES. EXPLOSIONS BY MISADVENTURE.

Both Brothers are fiddling with the windows on their heads.

"I get it," Shaker says. "You want me to do a ride-along. Work off my hours by sweeping up their dust. You realize what happened to my house is a miracle, too."

The Tullys mash around in their baggy moonsuits like slumland cosmonauts, communicating with each other through a secret vocabulary of masked muffle, subhuman grunts. The sofa sham and blanket that once underpinned Shaker seem to have vanished. The sun has grayed, and the clouds are cloudy. The Tullys stride for the truck, moving in real time, fidgety and graceless. For some reason, Shaker had expected the sensational slow-mo of professional athletes immortalized on vintage film stock.

He tries not to let the disappointment sour his evening.

*

Twilight, crickets, frostbite, and so forth. Shaker has fieldstripped a candy bar and now munches it under a dome of cosmic darkness. His legs and feet are dew-glazed into the yard. Mosquitoes in tactical formation are feasting on every inch of available flesh. Shaker has never been much of an outdoorsman, but recent events indicate he may have a potential career as a kind of vagrant survivalist or suburban bandito. He envisions himself trekking across deluxe USA tundra in a ski mask and camouflage poncho, shaking down paperboys for pocket change, heisting Girl Scout cookie deliveries. The fantasy culminates in a pack of angry villagers following a trail of snack crumbs up to the Hooster yard and discovering Shaker smeared in melted chocolate and peanut butter, an invasion of pigeons orbiting him in biblical indictment. Then lightning, a last judgment, a grudging rest. Maybe a grudging reincarnation, too.

For hours tonight, Shaker has stared at the gaping hole where he used to have a home. The Hooster girl does not appear. Shaker knows she's barricaded inside her bedroom, curled under the television's radiant beams, hiding herself away, and she's very right to be. He could visit. He could stand and walk the thirty impossible feet. He could even apologize for pity-fucking her mother and being pity-fucked in return. But he's too busy dwindling into smaller and smaller iterations of mopey, hamstrung anti-being.

This nonsense, he thinks, could be contagious.

Bandito or no, I am not healthy.

*

The woman confirms this. She appears an almost total replica. Pasta hair, pasty skin, overfond of mascara and rouge and chewing gum, some shyness in the bust. She has not changed enough. The bed sheet has returned, too, clinging Shaker around the throat like a limp eel. He unsnarls himself and sits upright. Maybe it's a lack of protein in his diet, or too much sloth, another fever image, the constant sun glaring down at him with disapproval.

Something is making Shaker hallucinate his ex-wife.

"California may have turned me stupid," she says, taking the blanket from him and rubbing the dirt off his cheek. "But Ohio has made you a hobo."

Now that his cheek is free of filth, she leans in for the coup de grâce. Shaker doesn't feel the kiss. He's too distracted with the wither and swell of his lungs, those sad, redundant organs ready to burst on their palsied vine.

"I think it's adorable and bold, what you've done with the place," she says, smoothing her skirt ruffles and twisting her mouth at the ex-duplex. "You don't see it much on the West Coast. But maybe in a few years, all the shanties will be knocked in half."

"Garrrr," Shaker says. "Garrrrr."

"Please, baby, no drooling."

Shaker is not conscious of it, but he has begun to sob. The cause is not splendor or sorrow or jealousy or relief. It is simply the announcement of inarticulate emotion as it comes burbling up the throat. He grabs back the blanket and stuffs it into his mouth, corking the surge, while she kicks her sandal through the pile of newspapers that demarcate Shaker and his vagrancy. She finds the weekend gazette, unfolds it to an inside spread, and shows Shaker a picture of himself standing pallid and zombie-faced in the background as Darb is torn from a huddle of EMTs, the house behind them afire.

"Do I really look that paunchy?" is the first intelligible thing out of Shaker's mouth.

She beams broadly, and that's when Shaker sees it. Or rather doesn't see it. Almost, he thinks. Almost.

"The eye makeup isn't right," he tells the woman.

"It's close."

"Close," he nods. "But not right."

"You would know," she says. "You're the husband."

"I was," he replies.

"And I am her. Our National Sensation. Live and in the flesh."

She holds herself at a practiced angle, hips going one way, flat chest the other.

Shaker groans. "You're an imposter, an impersonator. Birthday parties, bar mitzvahs."

"I do some retail business management on the side."

"Beautiful," Shaker says.

She gives him a wistful smile, a peek of her perfect teeth and the lone snaggly one. "But I had you going, didn't I?"

"Maybe."

"I've seen you walking around town and mowing yards and pedaling back and forth on that crazy teal bike. That one." Pointing at the Hooster's 5-speed on the porch. "What a pleasure to watch you work."

The woman rips his picture from the paper and tucks it inside her raggedy spinster's sweater. "Scrapbook," she winks.

"Don't suppose you have a name."

"Same as hers."

"Which one? She changed it so many times I lost count. Shouldn't you know that?"

The woman digs her sandal tip into the ground, scoops up some dirt, and flings. Shaker submits to the bombardment with a placid smile. She smooths her skirt again, but there isn't much skirt to smooth. "I really am from California. There wasn't a lot of opportunity for me out there. The professional doubles scene is glutted. I figured this quicksand patch of Ohio, she's the local legend, the territory would be ripe."

"This Ohio?" Shaker with a rude finger molesting the ground.

"My calculations were a little off." She picks around the rest of the newspapers, tearing coupons, lots of coupons.

"At least I found you," she adds, a melancholy catch in her throat.

"Me," he nods. "My purview."

"I was actually looking for a yard sale today."

"What luck," he says.

"Not luck. It's blind, stupid, perfect fate."

Shaker stirs his own leg through the newspaper pile, another leg, grabs some traction and tries to hold it, noticing the bed sheet has once again disappeared.

"Well, are you ready? I have to get back to Royce. He's almost due for his midday paste." The woman adjusts the heavy hang of wood beads on her neck and shakes her lush reams of strawberry blond hair, an unconvincing wig. "Let's get the mutton loaded before it begins to turn."

And using both arms, she drags Shaker by the scruff of his undershirt into the waiting car.

*

The mansion sits on the easternmost lip of town, beyond the shanties and ranches and occasional bulldozed duplex. Shaker has glimpsed the housing development in passing but never slowed long enough to peer around the scrub escarpment and iron gating to witness the luxury within. It's not much luxury anyway, no moats or tennis courts or helicopter ports, just an amplification of scale. Larger homes, larger lots. Also, larger failures. Of the twenty-plus properties on site, six are unfinished frames, eight don't have driveways, and five are nude plots of loam and clay. The remaining mansions are bundled together at the cul-de-sac end of the neighborhood. The woman's manor is a contemporary barrage of slanty angles and vertical glass, the type of home, Shaker imagines, that wouldn't survive a monsoon or mudslide. Looking around the incomplete landscape, however, it's almost as if the mudslide already occurred. The mansions have bloomed tumor-like from the rawness. Which is some kind of feat, thinks Shaker, softening to the idea.

They cross a crushed stone driveway and enter the manor, where the woman immediately scrolls down her top and airs her bare breasts.

"So?" she asks. "What do you think?"

Shaker, lost in the grandeur of a dirtless and mulch-less foyer, squints from breast to breast, breast to face, face to breasts. "Are tan lines a deal-breaker these days?"

"I mean my augmentations. I reduced two cup sizes and had them make the left one a little more lopsided. You've seen the real things. How do these stack up? Any tips or pointers?"

"Maybe if I—"

"No sampling the merchandise."

Shaker shrugs. "They look beach-worthy. Now the hair—"

"The hair is real. The lip mole. The tattoo. The flutter in my left eye. Real, real, real."

"She had special piercings," Shaker says.

"Draw them for me. Diagrams. I want diagrams."

"Are there tan lines down there, too?"

"You're disgusting."

"It is an art," he admits.

"But you're also much nicer than everyone says. The fumes and adhesives and chemicals must have cooked the meanness out of you."

"These days, I'm pretty much just frying grease." Shaker nods at his surroundings. "I am a man agog in a manor of agog."

"In that case, come meet the sweetheart," she says.

He follows her through a network of teak corridors into a barren library where a handsome man in a terry-cloth robe rests in a wheelchair, staring at a cold fireplace. Fiftyish, salt-and-pepper hair, royal bone structure, left eyebrow permanently arched. The woman wraps an arm around him and holds it there, as if steadying a nervous horse. "Say hi to Royce."

Shaker smiles mildly at the invalid.

"I'm serious," she says. "Say *hi* to him. He can hear everything. He's not a vegetable."

"Salutations," Shaker says, grasping the man's frozen hand and shaking it gingerly. He returns the hand to the armrest. No reaction of any kind. Shaker reaches again and massages the wrinkles from Royce's elegant lapels. "Seems a decent gent."

"He doesn't look stuffed to you?"

"Maybe a little stuffed," Shaker says.

"The poor guy," she sniffles.

"He's handsome at least."

"He's a vegetable!" she cries.

The woman squeezes Royce with both arms. Shaker is aware his own hands are twitching with intention, a need to grope. He pats Royce on the head and shoulder alternately, mesmerized by the expertly groomed layers of grayish hair.

"Does he get barbered often?"

"I know just how he wants it."

"You should open your own boutique," Shaker says, smooshing his face into Royce's coiffure. "You have a knack."

"My Rolls Royce, I call him."

"His hair smells good enough to eat."

"Oh, you should have seen him before the stroke." She separates Shaker from the Royce cranium. Then she leans down and awards the cranium a full-lipped kiss. "He made all his money as an amusement park magnate. The Whirler, the Heavy Turnip, the Lavender Monster. He built them all. It was the blood pressure medication that sent the clot up his brain. I found him on the floor of our gazebo with his pants wetted and his birding binoculars around his ears. Then we ran into some problems with the IRS."

"The Irish?"

She stilts herself on one leg, arms free and agitated.

"Yes, Mr. Shaker. It was the bloody Micks."

"I think I'm with the Dutch," Shaker replies meekly.

For this, he gets an annoyed eye-roll. The woman shifts her gaze to the hard oak floor. "It's difficult for an independent artist like myself to shake out a living these days. With Royce out of commission, I didn't have the best financial guidance. We had to blow out of California in a hurry. At least we have this house."

"I don't know if *house* is the word I'd—"

"Workwise, I'm in a dry spell until she puts out the next record. The release keeps getting delayed because her label is suing her for breach of contract. They say the new stuff is too experimental, too schizophrenic. She's not sounding enough like herself."

"I don't follow the gossip anymore," Shaker says.

"Once the album comes out, there will be an uptick in interest. There always is. The requests will start pouring in, I'll have steady work for a while, and then the adoration will dry up. Drought, flood, drought, flood. That's the cycle. It's sorta Old Testament."

"And Royce. What's he waiting for?"

"A miracle," she says quietly. "Any old miracle will do. For him, I'll wait forever. Ours is a love of substantial tilt."

Shaker sucks his bottom lip, tongue, lower teeth, the dopey expression that threatens to gormandize his entire face.

The woman tours him through the rest of the estate, from the empty fitness center to the empty sauna to a cavernous bedroom, also empty. *Mostly* empty. There is a plush king-size mattress on a frame so tall it almost rivals Shaker in height.

"We can set you up here in our auxiliary closet. It has a nice overlook of the neighbor's partly excavated pool. Plus, a bathroom and shower of your very own. You don't find that on most front lawns. Soap and shampoo, I'm afraid, are not included. Our stockpile is getting a little low."

"Everything is empty," Shaker says.

"We've sold off a lot of the embellishments, the incidentals."

"Is that what I am? An incidental?"

Shaker starts to haphazardly finger-flick the dirt crumbs and grass clumps off his trousers. Soon he is delivering wholesale smacks to his lower body and chest. The woman puts her hand upon him, slowing the operation of his arm.

Something long dormant inside the Shaker core quietly begins to quake.

"I really recommend you make fast friends with that shower," the woman says and walks out of the room.

*

When Shaker is fatigued from gazing at the dark crater of dirt in the neighbor's lawn and he tires of pacing the room's ivory rugs, he scales the high mattress and perches, legs dangling, on the ledge. Here is the view from the nosebleeds, and it is not so spectacular. Shaker has already showered four times. He's unable to doze. He probably couldn't eat any midday paste even if he was offered it. So he rappels off the bedside and searches the downstairs and backyard, where he finds the woman sunning herself inside a standalone greenhouse.

"I'm relocating to the basement," Shaker tells her. "That's more my kind of scene."

"It's mostly just retired appliances, broken furniture, and broken dreams down there. But suit yourself. I think there might be a foldup cot from Royce's convalescence. Everything else has been pawned."

"I didn't know anyone lived in these houses," he says.

"The neighbors are mostly nada," she replies, lifting a hand and pointing blindly at the miscellaneous smudges of world beyond the paneled glass. "That one and that one and that one are foreclosures. The developer went bankrupt. And thank god for that. We got the place über-cheap."

"Maybe there's some buried bounty in the other homes. Diamonds, silver, prissy show dogs and cigarette girls dipped in gold. Random loot."

"I think the drughead-junky-anarchist-squatters already plundered the good stuff."

She turns onto her stomach and aims a fingernail at a cream and brown Tudor-type monstrosity across the mud field. "Exhibit A."

"Looks nice enough. Like a piece of marble cake."

"Let's just say that we always lock our doors now. And our windows. And our lovely marijuana greenhouse."

"I thought that was herb I smelled."

"Our Tully friends have quite the green thumb for the stuff."

"You're on board with Tullys."

"They are fellow favor-traders."

"What's your favor?"

She gives him a sly grin.

"Tan lines," he nods.

"Don't be so gullible. I do bootlegs. Just to support me and Royce while I get my impersonation act off the ground. It's not the usual concert recordings and studio outtakes that always get pirated. We have our own special niche. Rehearsals, backstage chatter, bland conversations at the catering table, copyright hearings. I have some moles embedded in the entourage. There is a real economic opportunity in capturing the creative spaces that exist outside the art. The margins. The performance of nonperformance. Otherworldly residues, banal juices. Gossipy eavesdropped stuff."

"Are you recording me right now?" Shaker asks.

"Would that be a problem?" Another sly grin.

But Shaker is preoccupied, standing on toe tip at the greenhouse entrance and eyeballing the drug-squatter mansion. He cranes forward, licks his thumb and elevates it, divining wind direction, gale size, mushroom cloud circumference.

"What are you *doing*?"

"Estimating the blast radius," Shaker says and pockets his fist.

*

Even after the inferno, his cousin's property doesn't look much different. Same patchy grass and dead garden, dirt in piles, oaks so scrawny with skin disease they resemble cheap community theater scenery. Some fresh blackness rings the periphery and middle—mapping the reach of fiery debris, toxic fallout—but it's similar, too similar. Perhaps Shaker is hardened to the spectacle of apocalypse at home and yard. Maybe, in some cynical nook of his mind, he anticipated it all along. He lingers upwind from the disaster scene, feeling unbuoyed, a chronic prick in his throat. Then he remembers the paint mask on a string around his neck. He fits it to his face. The throat prickle is still there. Shaker discards the mask entirely and tries to breathe with only one lung. The left one. His favorite.

It is the third day of on-site cleanup, and the Tullys are down to the dark dregs. Shaker can only watch through squinched eyelids as the Brothers poach the rough ground with tongs and sandwich bags, pinching at things. The dominant wreckage has been towed. The bed of their truck brims with black baggies. Shaker is marking time on the sidelines with a plastic beach pail for any surviving alloys that might fetch a few bucks on the scrap resale market. He has not found any keepsakes. He hasn't even looked. Instead, he fantasizes about mainlining truth serum into each of his pores, defeating his liver with castor oil and a funnel, combusting under a million watts of American sunshine.

A Tully in his rubber hazmat gestures for the bucket. Shaker hops over a tire rut left by an emergency vehicle and extends the receptacle. A brass bolt grazes the plastic rim and lands with a satisfying ping. Shaker blushes with accomplishment. He holds himself aloft like an aristocratic statue in a public park. Then he lowers his beach bucket and dropkicks it across the property. The contents fly everywhere. On hands and knees he crawls the terrain, picking up the same scraps all over again.

*

In the truck, en route to the Tullys' private landfill, Shaker rides hump between the Brothers. The bucket is awkwardly wedged in his arms and jingling. The hazmat heads are off. Each Tully is ruddily cheeked, hair roostered up with sweat. They are taking turns at a can of diet soda Shaker conveys between them with his free hand. Driver Tully is the more muscular one. He has several terribly botched tribal tattoos sneaking up his neck and a chin dimple so prominent it could accommodate a golf ball. Navigator Tully is the weirder wit, the smirker, the schemer, Shaker's secret amigo. At least that's Shaker's benevolent assessment. The mufflerless truck fumes wafting in through the air vent might be making him a bit schmaltzy.

He swivels side to side, trying to address both Tullys. "So you guys remainder. Distribute bootlegs. You monopolize all the good winter work. Also, a little greenhouse agriculture. Half your tools have the town seal. Judging from the miles on the odometer, I'd say maybe some type of interstate traffic is involved. Here's an idea. The militia thing is a front." Shaker nods at each Brother. "Which one is the big, pink brain running the operation?"

The muscle shrugs. The smirker is no longer smirking. "You guys are good," Shaker says.

The Tully landfill is five square, squalid acres of singe and blemish with a children's nursery bordering one side and a graveyard the other. Shaker appreciates the symmetry. It lends an aura of life-spanning equilibrium the trash ruins do not deserve. As for the ruins themselves, Shaker is able to identify certain forms in the amalgamated slag, structures. A pipe stove, a Laz-E-Boy, swing sets, the crumpled tin roof of a detonated chicken shack. Shaker stands behind the truck and helps the Tullys dock the edge of the rubble. Once in position, the gate is unlatched, the shovels dispersed, and the three men begin the long drudge of scooping and flinging, flinging and scooping, pausing only to pocket the occasional bauble. This is how Shaker, near-blind under a borrowed pair of swim goggles and a rag around his mouth, finds Mortimer's gasmask. He lifts it by the straps, holds it up to his face. Peering into the empty eyeholes, he can't see anything of the boy. Only the reflection of a strange man, shifty and indistinct, waffling around on a lonely island of trash. Shaker grips the mask tighter. He is tempted to launch into a pseudo-Shakespearian monologue about guile, regret, blood oath and valor, and the tiny bronze drain at the center of the universe through which all living meat is eventually sucked.

He jiggles loose the silt and ash.

"Goddamn me," he whispers.

A few seagulls skim the landfill. Nothing settles. Shaker stashes the gasmask on the truck's dashboard and returns to his shovel.

The dregs don't get any darker than this, he thinks.

*

It's almost midnight when Shaker returns to Agog Manor and immediately aims for the upstairs bathroom so he can shower the dead smell off him. The water pressure is below par, inconsistent. He spends half an hour shivering under the trickle. Then he steps free of the stall and regards the towel rack. The towels are the lavish, swollen variety found in popular hotels and minimum-security prisons. Shaker is shy about involving himself in other people's laundry, so he tries to make a nude run for the basement. Hands cupped to groin, a trail of damp footprints behind him, he gets about three feet down the hall before he sees the master suite door is ajar. Shaker can't resist the lurid urge. He peers inside. The empty wheelchair is parked in the corner, and Royce is laid in bed. Someone has dressed him in safari pajamas. A herd of stuffed antelope and bovine surround his withered legs. Even so, Shaker senses a nobility about the man, an endurance and pride. He looks ready to star in his own series of gourmet coffee commercials.

Somewhere downstairs, a languid ballad is being played. Shaker follows the music to the garage and finds the woman sitting on a stool. She's staring helplessly at a ukulele on the workbench, her hands empty, while the soundtrack emerges from an old reel-to-reel unit. Noticing Shaker making puddles in the doorway, she clicks a foot pedal to halt the machine and shoots him a plaintive scowl.

"I think your gondola needs tuning," Shaker tells her.

"Long ago, I had this idea to make note-for-note re-creations of her entire repertoire. Every song, every album, every outtake. Even her bootleg conversations. Surely, there'd be a niche market for that, too. I could even make up a few lost albums, write them from scratch, and really add to the legacy. But I can't sing, can't play. I freeze up in front of microphones. I can't fake a single lick."

"Sounds familiar."

"But everyone knew you were a fraud. That was the charm. Your aloofness. That's what made it successful kitsch."

"My dog liked it," Shaker says.

"Even her rotten new stuff. Blenders, drum machines, car alarms. I can't get any of it right."

"She grew up in a suburban manor almost as posh as this, you know," Shaker says.

"So?"

"First, she copied the rustic trailer-park crap. Then she got bored and started copying the spazzy avant noise crap. She didn't invent anything. It's all vaudeville. An act."

The woman drops the ukulele in a bin filled with assorted percussionry: tambourines, maracas, egg shakers, Hare Krishna finger cymbals. "Of course you'd say that. I can see why she shot you in the chest."

"The chest-shooting thing was blown way out of proportion."

"You're bitter."

Shaker shrugs, his nudeness hid partially behind the doorjamb.

"Better acoustics inside the house," he tells her. "The high ceilings. The eighteen square miles of carpeting."

"But the American garage is a classic trope. It feels more authentically me."

She follows Shaker's gaze to the gargantuan SUV, black and glossed and ominously tinted behind her.

"One day, Royce and I are gonna drive down to Argentina. That's where the real pure sound is made now, deep in the rainforest where white parasites like us can't reach. Those people are untainted. They still yield to the image, the spectacle, the tropes. I don't think you would understand that kind of devotion."

Shaker shrugs again and again.

"Your name is too stupid to say with a straight face. Authority Shaker. My god. How do you manage?"

"I thought I was doing okay," he mumbles.

"And the nudist act?" she asks. "You're too good for our towels?"

"I want to lock them in a museum somewhere."

"Speak to me the way you spoke to her. The same language, the same voice."

"Isn't this already me?" Shaker asks.

"I don't see a scar on your chest."

"Maybe it never happened."

"What a stupid-looking chest. I bet you shave it. Do you shave it? You probably shave it."

The woman chews an indigo fingernail gone pale at the tip. "I will not backslide into your bed."

"Aren't all the beds here your bed?" Shaker asks.

She stops snacking on her nails and arranges her fingers into a pistol shape that she points at his hairless breastbone.

"Bull's-eye," she says.

*

122

The basement is a soundless, windowless vault, but Shaker can tell it's still nighttime on the other side of the dirt and the concrete. He can't sleep, can't not sleep. He slips back into his overbleached pants and stinky garbage shirt and wanders the manor like a bored prowler in sock feet. All the shadowy square footage spooks him more than his current bout of insomnia, yet he commits himself to remaining indoors and getting a fix on the situation. He barks himself all over the rich couple's insubordinate furniture. He returns downstairs. Minutes later, he's hoofing across the backyard in mud-soaked socks, a stolen maraca in his rear pocket.

Shaker meanders the suburban purgatory of half-finished properties and bare plots. He weaves among abandoned construction equipment, kicking aside the trash left by trespassers: energy drink containers and used condoms, pill vials, ripped underwear. The first house is stark and new, never occupied. The second is a foreclosure with childhood rumpus equipment and a push-mower grazing in the backyard. Shaker pauses at the mower, touches a finger to its cold engine, and awaits an emotional jolt that does not arrive. The next house is a skeletal frame. Shaker stands in what might be the living room area, totally exposed, with an anemic moon looming overhead and his trousers dropped, trying to unleash a hot, smoky piss on the hardwood. Unable to summon any flow at all, he stays rooted in his spot, tool in hand, aiming into the emptiness for what feels like hours.

On his return to the manor, he veers at the gates of the brown and cream Tudor. Only dull light in the windows, no sound, no junky squatters visible. Shaker presses against a side window that has been stripped of curtain and venetian slats. From this angle, he surveys assorted lawn chairs in the kitchen, a patio table with tropical umbrella, an inflatable pool stocked with dead fish. He moves to the next window and is startled by a face staring back: eyes large, hair amok, blubbery mouth. His own insomnia-crazed reflection. He peers past this gristliness into a room lit by television static. Positioned in a beach chair, the only audience for the TV screen's relentless snow, sits the Minnesotan. His body is pale and attentively upright, utterly distinguished except for the paper sign that is pinned to his sternum: *Hello! I'm Stinking Dead! Please Bury Me in the Minnesota I Probably Am Not Even From.* The note is secured to his lifeless chest with a spiny puffer fish, like a war medal.

And that's all Shaker needs to see of the brown and cream Tudor.

10.

Shaker has a savvy aptitude for siphoning fuel that utilizes a plastic tube inserted into his lips and a surfeit of sucking, spitting, sucking, etc., that climaxes in a brief bout of gasoline poisoning and bed rest. Once recovered, he is able to revive the abandoned mower and roar his narrow slices across the yard. The yard is flat and soft and practically grassless. Soon the machine, and Shaker behind it, are stranded in a foot and a half of mud sludge. Shaker yanks the mower's ripcord until the engine floods and the cord breaks. He tries to give the machine a hearty kick and loses his hiking boot in the muck. From the manor's bay window, he can feel them watching him. The imposter woman and her invalid husband. Shaker isn't upset about the surveillance. He just wishes there was something more captivating—like bloodthirsty wildlife or open-heart surgery, or some unholy combination of the two—for them to stare at all afternoon.

So far, he has gargled several flasks of mouthwash and a liter of cream soda. The rancid gasoline tang is still the only thing he tastes.

*

He dwindles through the ensuing day with one of Royce's leg blankets draped on his shoulders, a pair of pliers tucked in his waistband, something viscid snailing

125

down his left shinbone. He has sequestered himself indoors and avoids windows and natural sunlight. He examines his body for abnormal lesions and bruises that might symptomize divine wrath or foul play. The sun sets behind a horizon of unfinished homes, but Shaker doesn't see it. He's standing in the bathroom, sucking the blood he has bitten from his lip, baring his gorgeous pink fangs. Then he resumes his wandering of dark shoals until dinnertime.

They eat together at the long dining room table, the three of them laterally arranged so all individuals are spared direct sightlines. The woman spoons a pea-colored pesto into Royce's mouth with an impressive hook-armed technique that Shaker greatly admires. When she catches Shaker admiring her, he lowers his glance and takes another slug of his dank vinegar drink, which he is hoping will reduce the peppermint mouthwash's grotty aftertaste. He looks up and finds the woman glaring at him.

"One bonnet," he replies. "Many, many bees."

After the table has been cleared and Royce is wheeled off to his bath chamber for bubble-and-sponge hour, Shaker visits the upstairs library. He sits with the blanket over his head and phone.

"The ultimate misadventure," he tells the Tullys. "Probably best not to involve the authorities. Or the Irish."

The Brothers arrive after nightfall. Shaker stands watch on the street corner in one of Royce's brown velour jogging suits, Mortimer's gasmask on his face. Tullys One and Two enter the Tudor with a large gunny-sack. Ten minutes later, they exit hoisting an even larger sack. Shaker helps them heave it into the truck bed, and they pull him inside the truck, too.

Brother One unfolds the hanky in his fist. A squished puffer.

"A little late to name him," Shaker says.

They ride in silence until the landfill, where the trio handles the sack with the unhurried competence of part-time furniture movers, progressing deeper and deeper into the gray valley, searching for an inconspicuous area. Midfield, they dig. It doesn't take long to excavate a burial hole six feet in depth, the Minnesotan not having much width to account for. Shaker ratchets his gasmask hard against his face to create an airless suction, but he's still struggling to breathe. The landfill decay is full bore. The men set their shovels aside and roll the body into its snug and eternal chasm. Hesitantly, they regard the chasm, then one another, teeing up for a eulogy or group prayer. No one is very keen on removing his mask to speak. The Tully nearest Shaker elbows Shaker.

"Geronimo?" Shaker says.

The pallbearers-cum-gravediggers-cum-mourners-cum-priests trade pious nods and begin to rescoop the mud and ash and scoria, burying the Minnesotan in his sack.

Shaker is shoveling parts of appliances, caramelized fabrics, wire mangle and messy soot, a piece of electrical sprat, a plank inscribed with mystical runes—wondering if any of this is Mort—when the idea occurs. He lags at his shovel and gazes up at the blenched rim of moon, chewing on his big thought. One of the Tullys catches him dallying and beams him with a brick of wadded product. Shaker grumbles and starts shoveling again, but the idea is still with him the whole drive home and throughout the wordless goodbye, the hustle upstairs, the twenty-minute shower in which he forgets to incorporate soap and shampoo. It's all he can think about, this idea. Even when he's climbing out of the tub and realizes the woman is in the doorway, arms folded, chin jutting.

"Just stop it," she says.

"What?"

"You know what."

Shaker corkscrews his mouth until it is almost a vertical seam in his face.

"Oh, the wearing-my-stroke-victim-husband's-finery part, that's what. He's not your private mannequin."

"We're the same size," Shaker shrugs. "My going-to-town clothes got bulldozed. Do I really look so wrong in velour?"

She grabs the rumpled jumpsuit from the floor, sniffs it, and reels away. "This smells like dead cauliflower."

"The deadest," Shaker nods.

"I should warn you I sleep with a straight razor and strop underneath my nightie."

"Okay," Shaker says flatly.

"I once burned the nose off a petulant stalker using the cigarette lighter in a 1984 Plymouth Gran Fury. That was my nickname in college: *Gran Fury*. I've hung a chore list on the fridge."

"Just doing my due diligence."

"Shaker."

"I had an idea, a grand one," he shrugs.

And he squeezes past her, drenched and shivering and still very dirty, and locks himself in the basement.

*

The morning is not so kind. His coffee is bitter, the manor near-freezing, sunlight nil, and Shaker's idea is not grand at all. He's slumped over a bowl of untouched oatmeal in the breakfast nook with Royce. Both men are side-eyeing each other for vital signs, noxious spores, hot flashes, any meager display. Shaker feels ridiculous. His mind is only capable of shabbiness and obvious efforts. He takes affectionate hold of Royce's mouth and works him like a ventriloquist's dummy.

"I think you're a smart cookie, too," Shaker tells the man.

*

When he arrives, a roadblock has been constructed near the Tully homestead. Signal flares, sawhorse barricade, a spine of traffic rising up the steep hill's gravel lane. Each Brother is wrapped in an ammo belt with concussion grenades dangling like holiday ornaments. Their shotguns are shouldered and safety locked at least, and they have Old Glory do-rags wrapping their lower faces. Shaker has previously heard rumors about militia traffic stops in this backwoods region but never witnessed one himself. He parks off-road and moves around the convoy on foot, studying the faces of anxious and irate motorists. Tully One is alongside the lead vehicle, a shark-finned coupe with suicide doors and a hazardously beehive-haired lady at the steering wheel. Brother Two is foraging around the open trunk, filled entirely, it seems, with pink cosmetic cases. The lady flashes a faceful of panic at Shaker while, at the rear of her car, Brother Two scrutinizes a jar of epidermal cream.

"Looks like plastique, ma'am," Shaker says.

Brother One ignores Shaker's comment and waves the woman around the barricade as his sibling hurriedly retrofits all the tubes and balms and froths into their original comportment. Tully Two gives a menacing glare to the next car in the queue, then shifts the menace to Shaker, tempering it somewhat.

"Guess the militia stuff is genuine," Shaker says. "Protecting the homeland from the hippies, the harpies, the brownies, and the blood of King David. What a bummer."

One and Two reorient their stances, thumbs hooked into their bandoliers. They rally together a terse moment, then turn to Shaker and nod at the truck. Shaker in turn points to the suburban utility tank he has borrowed from the manor and parked at the end of the caravan.

"It's not the truck I want to take," he says.

*

By his twelfth attempt, Shaker has devised an intricate method of hopscotching both feet into the hazmat at once. The action is akin to holstering a rare and impractical firearm. He worms into the armholes, zips himself crotch to chin, and latches his head. Instant cosmonaut. Shaker acclimates to the alien sensation of so much stiff rubber and disorganized mass flush against his skin. His center of gravity has mysteriously traveled somewhere near his kneecaps. He stumbles about druggedly through the landfill with exaggerated strides, slow-growing confidence. Then he realizes he has forgotten his shovel. He looks around, but there's no similar tool on site. So Shaker uses his clunky boots to dislodge the impacted rubbish. He kicks up a shower nozzle fused to a toilet seat, a coiled garden hose, three milk crates smelted into one grated gob. These he carries to the flattest range of the landfill, careful to avoid the Minnesotan and his pauper's hole. Shaker lays out the recoveries in deference to era and size and structural integrity. He is conscious of color scheme, too.

He does find a bone, a single one, maybe a femur. Too old to be the Minnesotan. In the same area is a scattering of Indian arrowheads. Shaker brushes them off, holds them to the light, and casts them aside with a shrug.

The next round results in a malformed tuba, several roller-skate wheels, a piddle of liquefied marble, and a teddy bear doll. There are rosary beads and abstract glasswork, forged diplomas, ninja chucking stars, a postal receptacle, a lamp, crack pipe, denture jaw, ceramic bust of Sigmund Freud, a gerbil's exercise gyroscope, skimp-black lingerie with accompanying fishnets. Shaker has laid it all into row and is now clearing out a clean swath. The center, the axis, the base. He hastens off to the SUV, filching an incomplete wrench set and saddlebag along the way, and returns with the span of baling wire he purchased from Softy's on store credit. This he stretches around the postal box and tuba and toilet-nozzle, bricking them together on the cleared ground. He reinforces the base with a cordon of chicken mesh.

Shaker concludes by crossing over the trash reef that encircles his little project. From this short distance, he regards the stump of wire and scorched debris he has made. He nods approvingly and thinks:

Perhaps I have not embraced ridiculousness enough.

*

But then the rest of the day happens. Shaker paces around Agog Manor with nothing to stack up, nothing to mow, and he can only avoid the garage for so long. He resorts to stuffing his head with cotton and tufts of torn shirt, but he can still hear the music, an endless bluegrass dirge that has yet to proclaim its capital topic. He unstopples an ear and listens closer. The voice is male, an old-timey recording disturbed with hiss and grit. Shaker cannot take the grit very seriously. He replugs his ear, clomps into the bathroom, and crams his skull under a running faucet.

"Shaker," he burbles to himself, "you are making a scene."

He joins Royce on the patio deck. The invalid is bundled in a children's beach blanket that advertises a cartoon varmint franchise Shaker barely remembers from his youth. Shaker sits on the patio railing, amateurishly baptized and drip-drying in the chill night air, his back to the yard, reviewing the man. When the woman abandons the garage and comes out, too, he has reduced his mind on the matter.

"Absolutely not," she replies, worrying a stick of nicotine gum into her mouth.

"He needs it. The pj's, the prune juice. Look how pasty he looks. The manor is turning him albino."

"Royce stays with me."

"Then you come, too."

"Me? I spent my afternoon parading around a bail bondsman's office Christmas party, getting my muumuu tugged, my muffins groped. I did my whole lip-synch spiel, tried to sign a few autographs. Nobody knew who I was supposed to be. They wouldn't even cover the cab fare home. If I ever leave the house again, it will be inside a body bag. A sexy, cashmere body bag. Hot funeral pink."

"How about a gunnysack?" Shaker asks.

"That would work, I suppose."

"Let me take him."

"No," she says.

"Thank you."

"Wait, what?"

"I'll have him back by midnight."

"I didn't say—"

But Shaker is already wheeling his catatonic cargo towards the car.

*

The Regal Beagle's newly remodeled entrance is the type of slipshod hotchpotch Shaker can imagine an indebted drunkard such as himself being compelled to manufacture under gunpoint and duress. The door is battered and does not hold to its frame. The steps are not handicap accessible. Shaker nervously eyes Royce and his sizeable contraption. He wheels him backwards twenty or so feet. Then he gets a running start, attains supersonic speed, and rams the chaired man upward and through.

Tonight is a weeknight, and the Howitzer is not on duty. The jukebox is off. The only commotion is Royce's wheelchair crunching peanut shells and sand as Shaker glides him to a table in the darkest corner of the room. They settle in. Shaker notices a few curious looks and belches, but no one approaches. The Beagle hasn't changed much. The same dartboard and fire-code citations next to the ladies room, a fresh snarl of antlers protruding from the trophy wall. Royce is attired in a cowboy shirt complete with pearl buttons and filigree stitching, and the crease in his hair has been abolished; instead, the whole gray mass is swept upright and shellacked with glamour gel. Shaker has inflicted a similar effect on his own head and swivels it in the wall-length mirror, admiring himself and Royce in their polished hairstyles and matching shirts.

"Buckaroos," Shaker tells Royce, leaning forward to align the prone man's collar. "Don't let anyone tell you different."

Amid this primping, Tobin slides from his post at the bar and comes over. Shaker says, "A round of prune juice for me and my ranching friend, please."

"The circus was last week," Tobin replies.

"Sure was."

"Two clowns gone missing."

Shaker nods at this, hands flat on the table so as not to disturb the mound of pompadour weighing down his brain like a brick. He opens his mouth and carefully speaks with it.

"My dogs are gone, my duplex is gone. My futon, my lamp, the single page of crinkled porn I kept taped to the tissue box for convenience. All that domestic splendor pretty much vacuumed from my life. At least grant a condemned man his beverage."

Someone has engaged the jukebox. A subwoofer is pushing subterranean frequencies through the floorboards, rattling the car keys and asthma inhaler in Shaker's pocket. He can't help it. He scratches the cold cement hair. It feels like a prehistoric crustacean latched on his scalp, harmless and endangered. He looks up from the table. Tobin has lifted his own oval head, nodding it cautiously, as if the thing is overloaded with nitroglycerine.

"A couple prune juices," Tobin says.

"That's right."

"I'll see what we have in the fridge."

After the bartender is gone, Shaker turns to Royce. "That whole life? The one I was persecuted for? Feels like another person's life anyway. You're standing trial for moral depravities you don't remember committing, so how do you know other people are remembering it correctly? I'm sure I've forgotten some good stuff, too."

Shaker huddles in, fixing Royce's blank stare in his own.

"It wasn't much of a heyday," he whispers. "I woke up with a lot of headaches and hernias and always the same nameless woe. There were moments, I swear, the *glue* seemed to be sniffing *me*."

Royce's tongue is licking the dehydrated rim of his lip, trawling it, and Shaker senses a suppressed accusation in the act.

He shrugs a few times, upsetting his haircut again.

"How ridiculous is too ridiculous? I'm not making mountains out of mashed potatoes or trying to find off-street parking for the mothership to land. The mothership isn't *coming back*." Shaker digs around the pretzel bowl and pops a twisty into Royce's mouth. "I may have blowed it up."

After three-four drinks in happy solitude, Shaker is preparing to wheel Royce out the door when Tobin approaches again. He has a manila folder with him.

"Do you like the new door?" he asks.

"Needs a ramp."

"It took me a couple days to rebuild," Tobin says. "Had to close the bar on a holiday weekend. Lost a lot of money."

Shaker buttons his coat, shoots his cuffs, then repeats the arrangements on Royce. "You did a wonderful job."

"Thanks."

Shaker looks up. "I was talking to my gimp."

Tobin smiles. "That door was fucked beyond repair, man. The glass was shattered, frame smashed. Some idiot tried to set it on fire."

"It's just a door," Shaker replies.

"Did you really think you'd get away with it?"

"Huh?"

Tobin opens the manila folder. "Security camera across the street."

He fans the photographs across the tabletop, a dozen blurry images. Not blurry enough. Shaker leans over and pretends to examine them, but his eyes are closed. His mouth is still struggling to process the prune juice's bitter-salty aftertaste.

"You're a lucky dude," Tobin says. "The Howitzer has been helping me locate my special Zen place. I'm a new goddamn man. Just call me Mr. Arts-and-Crafts-and-Prozac. I can't say everyone shares this philosophy. We have some mutual friends who prefer to remain anonymous. Maybe they think you've suffered enough, they packed up their catapults, and all is forgiven. Or maybe their silence is a way of making you suffer more."

Shaker glances around the Beagle. Six men at the end of the bar are staring into their empty beer steins, pretending not to listen. Shaker performs a quick touch-up on Royce's head.

"So we're all good here?" he asks.

Tobin smirks. "Just as long as you don't mind a little revenge piss in your prune juice."

He rubs Royce's haircut all out of profile and returns to his slot behind the bar, where he swallows several green pills and picks up a clump of yarn, a pair of knitting needles.

Shaker leans low and whispers into Royce's ear, half-hidden by gel crust and shag. "I think we won that round."

Shaker carts Royce to the car, hefts him and belts him and gets the wheelchair loaded, and soon his high beams are roving across the smooth knolls of ruin at the Tully landfill. Fog has moved in, a morbid touch. Shaker rolls up to the stump. Lit solely by headlamp and misted, the exact origin of the materials bound in chicken mesh remains a mystery. But there is texture and inclination, an elemental quality, and that's all the origin Shaker needs. He fixes Royce in his wheelchair at the far end of the flatness, so if anything pitches over the invalid won't be collaterally damaged. The man's useless legs are layered in flannel blankets. Shaker has tied a handkerchief around Royce's face. Satisfied with the arrangement, Shaker hopscotches into the hazmat, fires up a flashlight and produces a shovel, and resumes his slow toil on the stump, which, seen from Royce's distance and grayed in mist, is beginning to lean slightly to the left.

11.

Shaker in nocturnal chrysalis: unclothed, sleep mask dangling off an ear, mouth ajar with maximum drool. This is his regular slumberful state. Except he is standing upright. Sometime after midnight, she wakes to the noise and finds him in the kitchen. He's shifting foot to foot, the linoleum lisping under his bare, sticky feet.

"You sleepwalk?" the woman asks under her kabuki skin cream, her hair in spools.

Shaker, eyes shut, blindly points at the oven door that is open.

"So you're either preparing an invisible soufflé or you're trying to gas yourself to death," she says. "Or maybe you're about to explode the whole bodega."

"Mmmmm."

"It's not *your* bodega!"

She tugs a hank of his hair. Lazily, his eyelids flap open. Shaker feels furcated, half in this room, the rest evaporated, lost to the wind, a molecular frenzy.

The woman sighs and shuts the oven door and tromps back to bed.

It's not a *bad* feeling, Shaker thinks.

12.

Shaker's initial lapse into semi-sobriety came
several years previous in a midsized arena strung with
athletic association banners and patriotic bunting and
beer sponsorship logos. He was keeping his head together
at the time with a few protean substances stored in a
sporty toolbox. The toolbox was clutched under his arm
as he stood on the arena floor with his nostrils sticky, his
skull bombed. Only six or seven other people were on
the arena floor with him. The rest of the vast space was
empty. The audience milled around in the emptiness,
watching Shaker's ex-wife writhe around on stage in an
oversized cassock, lost in lumps of massive fabric. This
was the first and only time Shaker had seen her since the
divorce. She was chanting into an air traffic controller's
headset, babbling in tongues, dry humping the stage,
her eyes rolled to the whites. The usual shamanic shtick.
Her backing musicians, The Meek American Rapture,
were mostly scabs and ringers in this incarnation. They
bludgeoned their instruments with sharp implements
and power tools but not much passion, lolling in and out
of narcoleptic spells.

Shaker, his eardrums stuffed with shredded sanitary
napkins, gazed up into the blaze of lamps and random
halos, the endless heat on his face, seeing spots.

He walked over and tapped the shoulder of the nearest patron, thirtysome feet away, and said, "I see spots."

The kid had to tweeze out an earplug to hear Shaker. But Shaker was whipping his head around too much, trying to knock the splotches from his vision, and missed the kid's response. There was a smoke machine on stage, and the smoke was everywhere. When Shaker's eyesight cleared, the kid was gone.

On the side of the stage, Shaker could see his ex-wife's husband. The man stood about six foot six, tailored shirt sucked into a crisp pair of khakis, collar buttoned at the jugular, no tie. Both benefactor and manager, he rented the arenas for her, the tour buses, the union crew, bought airtime on radio and TV. He even bankrolled the greasy tabloid notoriety. Shaker, it seemed, was the only person in this artificial ecosystem not receiving some form of brownbag payola, and he felt a little excluded, a little nixed. His ex-wife had become one of those public-domain punchlines that linger in the netherworld of quasi-fame, dazed and hostile, although she had her adherents, a tiny but venerated gaggle of contrarian critics. There were several in every college town, every city. They penned jargony screeds that argued her unlistenable music was a subversive indictment against the capitalist privilege that had landed her on all those rented stages. In this version of events, she was a courageous dissident, a pop-culture saboteur, and not just a poseur art-nut subsidized by her very rich husband.

After the eleventh encore, she was ushered offstage by a cartel of leather-clad teamsters and unpaid interns. The overhead lamps ignited, and the arena was reshaped around a dense smog that hung like a diseased brain above the remaining audience. There were only three of them now, small and squint-eyed. Her set had lasted seven and a half hours. A single custodian came out onto the floor with a dustpan and broom, looked around, shrugged, and disappeared behind the service door.

Shaker, still maneuvering under his glue stupor, felt shriveled by the spectacle. His legs were sore. A metallic flavor filled his mouth. Twin security men with the close-cropped facial hair of silent film villains were stationed in the doorway, sharing something dainty in a roach clip. Shaker gave them the money in his wallet, then gave them the wallet, and they awarded him a handful of mushroom caps, which he gobbled all at once.

"Bon voyage," a twin said.

"I am a pillar of salt," Shaker replied. He touched his left pectoral, knuckled it, squeezed. His eyes were misting. "I feel *thick*."

Shaker used his shirtsleeve to blot the wetness from his forehead and face. "What are these socks doing on my feet?" he asked.

"You don't look so good, guy. What other garbage you been taking?"

"All of aisle nine," Shaker smiled.

He hefted the toolbox of inhalants, weed killers, sink cleansers, fluorescent cosmetics, household toxins. The tubes were crushed flat, the sprays depleted.

Shaker buckled at the knees. The only activity in the entire arena was his body smacking glorious concrete.

"Touch me," he moaned. "Someone please just touch me."

He woke in a hospital bed three days later, feeling fine, absolutely fine. He had sweated all the sensation—national or not—out of his broken body, flushed his nervous, nervous system, the chemicals and the need for the chemicals. All of it purged. The doctors told Shaker they'd never seen adult nasal passages so hairless and clean.

His ex-wife never paid him a visit, although one of her roadies arrived with a much-abused tuba jammed full of yellow carnations. She didn't bother to include a card.

Now here she is in Agog Manor, at least someone eerily derivative of her, and Shaker can't tell if he is experiencing the same need or something new. Royce is slumbering upstairs, deposited in his sheets with a year's worth of financial glossies banked around him. The greenhouse is dark. All life in the manor feels tranquillized, embargoed. Shaker hasn't showered off the garbage smell yet. He's standing in the doorway, the reek pulsating off him in concentric rings. The woman is stripped to her slip and sitting in front of the cold fireplace, scouring her hair with a tortoiseshell brush. Her legs are bruised and unshaven. Shaker recognizes the purple tattoo of a coiled serpent that crests her inner thigh. She stops brushing but doesn't turn around. She only holds up the tortoiseshell, as if passing off a track-and-field baton.

"Do the back," she says.

"Isn't it long enough you can reach yourself?"

"Don't be a boob," the woman replies.

Shaker kneels behind her and accepts the brush, performing a few practice rakes on his own head, and then he begins taking great whacks at hers. He runs through the strawberry blond curls, going with grain and against, until he feels something loosen, a tension unturn. He touches her neck; the skin seems to vibrate. He is aware a low-grade euphoria is blooming throughout his body, and he grudgingly submits to it. Then the woman starts to hum a familiar melody, an old outtake, a forgotten favorite. Shaker goes rigid. He tries to bung shut his ear canals by sheer force of will, but that only magnifies the lovelorn burn that's being generated in his loin region. Grudgingly, he submits to this, too. Just as he is getting used to the humming, it trails off. Her hair is soft and tamed. Shaker sucks in a desperate breath as she leans backward, fitting her contours to his, their bodies molded, neither of them making any sound at all.

The only real surprise here, Shaker realizes, is how much the silence hurts his ears.

13.

Shaker regains consciousness in a new decade, mummified in crepe paper and holiday tinsel, confetti flakes in hair. He's lying in an empty manor room he doesn't recognize, and its ceiling is bearing down on his headache with an industrial clang. The woman is somewhere on the same floor. Shaker can hear the rustling of her obscenely-sequined party dress, the one she has been wearing for days and has half-picked to pieces and scattered like fairy dust around the upstairs. They are a week after New Year's. Outside, a steady escalation of high snows and entombing ices. Shaker touches his head. Someone has given him a very short and unflattering haircut.

Since mid-December, he has toured the regular haunts, and no one has tried to assassinate him yet. He has weekly check-ins with the Tullys. No explosions to clean or corral. All the citizenry have gone docile and seem to be keeping their fantastic disasters safely indoors, or else have shipped them somewhere out of state.

The stump. It has grown into a stack. The Ohio winter, however, has not been gentle. Each day, Shaker is outside in borrowed hazmat and parka, re-wrapping the chicken wire, re-bundling the trash, trying to maintain a respectful structure ten feet in height. A garbage spine that will someday breach the tyranny of heaven. He keeps a ladder at the landfill. When the snows lift and the wind lessens, he mounts the rungs and adds a few more pieces—an appliance, a copper orb—as if crowning a Christmas spruce. But Christmas has passed and his energy is flagging. Today, Shaker finds the structure's topmost amalgam has been sheared off and blown westward forty feet. The monument is eroding grain by grain. His struggle is a constant glacial slog against a winter that is no better.

One morning, the Tullys appear at Agog Manor with a gift box strapped in red ribbon. Both Brothers are sunburned and pruned from a southerly vacation. Shaker rips into the box and unfurls a new hazmat of his very own.

"Guess you want the other one returned," he says and suits up. His fingers fill the unknuckled hands. Head occupies hood. Perfect fit.

The Tullys gesture towards the truck outside. A drive, they want.

"Where you wanna go?" Shaker asks, already knowing. He takes a moment to luxuriate inside his weatherproof self, inhaling the plastic fabric that makes his nostril hair tingle and stand at attention. That familiar delirium of synthetic smells. He's immersed in it. Shaker follows the Brothers to their truck, trying not to huff too loudly.

When the truck rolls into the landfill and parks at the clearing, he doesn't bother to feign surprise. All three men exit the vehicle and traipse toward the structure. Dirty snow dandruffs the ground. The monument leans against its fresh cable moorings. Shaker tries to remain casual, but soon he is stopped in his tracks, squinting hard, an intent look.

"Fuck me," he says in his sharp rasp. "At this angle, it looks like a big, gray dong."

Shaker stews in the frigid breeze while one of the Tullys drags a ladder to the stack and pries free a toolbox that is stamped with the town seal. Shaker's hood is fogged with bad breath, his whole suit overripe.

"Still, you gotta admit," he says, "I've done worse work."

Tully One returns with his toolbox, and the men resume their initial position, ranked three-across with arms folded and surveying the monument, like physicists in an underground bunker awaiting some luminous detonation. The wind heaves around them, and the monument sways.

The Brothers slowly nod.

*

Shaker gives it struts. He gives it gradations. And every morning after breakfast, he sweeps away the pack of homeless men who have begun to congregate around his project in nomadic camps. Then he works through the afternoon, planing the sides, squaring the stack off, rendering it less penile in appearance.

The homeless men are not many, and they usually come in clusters, sometimes pairs. Shaker can see the caravan of them stretching up the trash dunes, a row of shabby cloaks, tangled moss beards. A dozen silent faces, stony and old. He thinks maybe they are on some type of scavenger mission, so he stands protective of his land of junk, but the tramps never filch a thing. And they seem to be surviving fine without masks or hazmats, which leads Shaker into a reverie about garbage zombies and scrap-hoarding specters, the junk land as graveyard, the graveyard as world.

The daydream inevitably deflates, and Shaker returns to his trash project, which he will soon unveil for public ridicule. Shaker had originally envisioned a series

146

of matched monoliths rising from the apocalyptic ash like a fire-ravaged Stonehenge for future generations— the homeless and the sheltered—to ponder and debate and maybe, too, immortalize on commemorative dinner plates. But it's the aloofness, the aloneness, that seems truer to the spirit that undergirds Shaker's creation as it stands strutted and straightened in the January chill. And also seems truer to Shaker's niggling, unresolved guilt. So he decides this is the one, the only one. His masterpiece. It's nearly ready. Just a bit of burnishing on the top face and edges.

And then the far fringes of a nor'easter arrive and knock the monument sideways into the dirt, and Shaker must begin the slow build all over again.

*

She tries her hair up, tied in a mass like an animal nest, or else long and drapey, twisted in rolls, upheld in clips. Sometimes wigs: noir black, bark brown, the same strawberry blond as her actual hair. She swaps the patchwork muumuu for a leopard-skin leotard, a snowy-colored cultist's gown, nudie suit, farmer's flannel, S&M corset, with cowgirl hat and without. She spins in the mirror and catches Shaker peeking over her shoulder, a slinky confusion in his look.

"People love to bicker over authenticity," she says. "But, by my lights, the only authentic act is fakeness. The transparently plastic. That's the only honesty left."

"Is that? Is that...?" Shaker creeping closer.

"Shark's jaw."

"Thought so."

"Custom made. The whole necklace. A perfect replica."

"Smells fishy."

"Ha."

"I can't smell much anymore," he shrugs.

"All her phases, all her shadows. I can inhibit each of them at any given time, without scheme or logic, just like her, exactly like her. The trick, I think, is she doesn't know herself. That's the key to true originality."

"Probably gets exhausting," he says. "That shark jaw looks heavy."

"You think I must have had a sad childhood."

Shaker nods.

"Of course I had a sad childhood! You know the story. A young girl sits with a radio. She's hiding under a dingy blanket, or she's alone in the backyard, she's at some abandoned gasworks or church basement or the cemetery behind her school. It's the same sadness everyone else suffers, but hers is more...cinematic, I guess. Mythic. She turns the radio on. She adjusts her chunky headphones, the geeky glasses that are too big for her geeky face. She waits for that song that's going to save her lonely, little life. And if not save it, at least fool her into thinking her life shines a bit brighter, has some special luster. And the funny part? This lifesaving song? It's going to come along and ruin her forever. All her romantic expectations will be so warped, she'll live in a continual state of heartbreak and disappointment and misanthropic funk for the rest of her days."

The longer Shaker stares at the woman, the less he's sure what he sees. The bouffant wig that rises like a grain silo. The miniature anvil earrings, the shark bone on a rope around her neck. All these impounded *parts*.

"I no longer know or care what's natural," she says. "We are all surrogates for something or someone. People make holes in the world, and other people fill them."

"How does it work?" Shaker asks. "These jobs you do?"

"Someone calls me on the phone. I drive over. I dress up, lip synch, prance around, die of embarrassment. Then someone uses a spatula to pry me off the floor, hands me my crumpled clothes, and I go on my merry way with a few dirty dollars in my pocket."

"I guess it beats jumping out of a cake," Shaker says.

"The strangest thing is I can't even remember the first time I heard her. One day, I just woke up and realized she was everywhere. Like she'd always been there, lurking in the corners, speaking my secret thoughts, saying what I didn't know I felt. It can almost make you paranoid, knowing someone like that is out there."

She sucks in a sniffle, lowers her face, and sops up the tears with the fringe of her granny shawl.

"When I mouth her words, when I do that crazy epileptic dance she does, when I'm pretending to be all the hers that have ever existed, or will ever exist, it's not mimicry at all. It's a channeling, a communion. It's like a séance with myself."

A troubled grin flares across her face. "My body becomes a language only the dead can speak."

*

Hob Brock sits at the shopping mall kiosk in a forward hunch, hands steepled, a new goatee around his mouth. The kiosk is set up between a Finish Line shoe store and a store that sells headstones and vanity grave markers, also named Finish Line. Hob has held this chair all winter, peddling sunglasses to kleptomaniac preteens and minivan moms. The mall's tile floor looks both glisteningly clean and salaciously soiled. The jingles on the public address system are neutered versions of pop songs that have not been relevant for several presidential administrations. These surrounding sounds and odors make Shaker nostalgic for all the muggy hours he squandered in similar food courts as an adolescent. Maybe it's a type of homesickness, this clinched thing inside him. A single sheet of glass hangs too distant above.

"You wanna try anything on?" Hob asks.

"I'm sorry?" Shaker replies.

"You working?"

"I am not."

"Fucking sunglasses," Hob says.

"I like the mirror ones. They'd look good on you. Like a stuntman. A movie cop."

Hob shakes his head, folds shut the beach novel in his lap, and gives Shaker a well-rehearsed stink face.

"It will be spring soon," Shaker says.

"Fancy that."

"Yes," says Shaker, the restless transient, starting to smile. "I am fancying it from afar."

"You bother me, brother."

"Both of us." The smile on Shaker's face is wide enough to wrap around his head until the corners tie together, like strings on a cheap mask. "My phone number has changed. I have my own shower now. Just so you know. I read in the paper Ms. Blaudin died a happy old woman of ninety-four."

"Heart failure," says Hob.

"Very sad thing."

"For most of us."

"I might be in the market," says Shaker, flashing a credit card that is not his, "to buy some sunglasses after all."

*

Shaker cannot smile such benign idiotism at the woman in the kitchen who is taking apart a robust cabbage with a rectangular meat cleaver. Jettisoned food scraps are stuck to the back-splash tile. Her technique is mean and brusque. Shaker holds himself a generous distance away from her whacking arm. The longer he stares at the mutilated vegetable, the more it seems to assume the spoiled features of his own crinkled face. He gulps hard and locates the cutting board, dirtied, in the sink. Just in case he needs to shield himself against any wild swings.

"Such a beautiful head of hair," she says.

"Mine?"

"That was the first thing I noticed about you. That lush mound. It was only later, much later, that I realized there were eyes-nose-mouth in that pale potato."

Shaker resists the temptation to reach up and inspect said parts. Then he relents, and indeed the pieces are there. They are still not smiling.

"Sometimes I dream of scalping you," she says. "Wearing that lush hairpiece on a nice rope around my neck. Along with the shark jaw."

She smacks the knife downward, bits of greenery spewing everywhere. "Why don't you wash some dishes?"

"Are those teeth marks?" Shaker mulling the countertop.

"It's good to keep tabs on the people who adore you so much they may one day murder you." She grins this while twirling her very large knife. Shaker steps up, steps back.

"You're feeling unwell," he says.

"Pardon me, sweetie?"

"I'll say it again. Just put down the tomahawk."

The woman sinks the knife into the green mound, ventilating the vegetable, and she shakes her free hands at him. Shaker picks up a dish and runs it under the faucet several times without applying any soap. He's waiting for the moment to cling, shimmy, become moon-shaped.

"I must be missing something," he says. "All the great blitzes of yesteryear that went straight up my nose. Damaged the ol' radar dish."

She snatches the saucer from him and appears ready to hurl it. "I've seen pictures! All the hours you've spent secretly gallivanting around that stupid dump with my husband!"

Shaker puckers his expression with such vehemence he can feel his capillaries crack. "Which Tully told you?" he asks.

"I needed to know why Royce comes home smelling like compost."

"The smell's not so awful."

"You realize, of course, you're making me revise all the wonderful principles I've always held about outsider art."

Shaker blinks but not simultaneously. One eye, the other eye. An unnerving tic for unnerving times.

The woman sets down the dish and is now touching him on his forearm's juncture, the thinnest, weakest, most Shaker-like part of him. "Play your role. Stay on script. You're still one of my husbands."

"Your impotent harem."

"Yes," she nods.

"Yes," he nods, too.

"Shaker."

"Yes." He's still nodding.

"The Shaker I know does not build mysterious things in scummy, ostracized places." She takes her hands off him and wipes them and cups her breasts, molding a provisional cleavage of that pale-freckled flatness. "Remember this?"

"Don't be nasty," says Shaker.

"Sometimes I'm nasty," she shrugs.

"Then be nastier, much nastier."

Shaker takes a long, chaste breath and leaves the kitchen as the knife gets going again. In the garage, he suits up, sidestepping the crush of instruments and frayed mic cables on the floor. He observes his funhouse reflection in the SUV's black paint: a squat, elasticized moonman henpecking his various freedoms and shackles. Shaker gets into the truck and guns it around the cul-de-sac and main neighborhood road, too depressed to admire all the glorious rubber melt he has left streaked across his blighted half of the hemisphere.

A monotone of gray winter clouds. Sunlight laminates the seams. There isn't enough brightness to require sunglasses, but Shaker thinks wearing them would improve his mood. Unfortunately, the forty pair he purchased from Hob are sitting in a shoebox under his cot, and his facemask is only vaguely tinted. Shaker tries the radio and tunes in an opera. A male baritone is plundering his diaphragm for a note so low it rattles the vehicle. Shaker steers with his knee, trying to slice the stereo's EQ. He can't stomach this much orchestra in the morning. So he roves the dial, only half-listening. He's more interested in the unusual smell that has followed him from the garage. Shaker clicks off the radio and winces through the sudden windshield glare. Gold everywhere. Cat food, he thinks. The car smells like cat food.

"Driver," intones a familiar voice from the backseat. "Mind the speed limit, please."

Shaker struggles to spin round, expecting to see Royce handsomely buckled in his suede chinos and refurbished with speech. But it's not Royce. Nor is it Thin or Hob or the Howitzer, nor a homeless man in gray monk robes. He's wearing a ridiculous yellow lounge-lizard suit and a too-short crew cut that almost matches Shaker's own, an athletic duffel on his lap.

Shaker has slowed the SUV to a mild carom. He's trying to nod hello.

"Jailbird flies free," Darb says and reaches forward to straighten Shaker's head towards the road.

"Am I pale?" Shaker asks their glassed reflections. "I feel pale."

"Sorry if I made you brown the pants of your snowsuit. That would be a shame. Suppose I got a knack for this sneaky stuff. Maybe I could be a private investigator. Keep law and order intact. Wouldn't that be a reversal?"

There's no more movement in Shaker's head. He says nothing. Darb leans forward and whispers into Shaker's ear, "I said wouldn't it?"

"Guess so," replies Shaker.

Satisfied, Darb leans back and continues. "It'd be long hours. Sit in a car. Watch out the window. Pee with your equipment in a pickle jar. This arid weather just parches me, man. But you guys got lots of climate control inside that greenhouse, yeah? The twenty-car garage and so on. Interesting how the tables do turn. Swively tables, I guess. Roulette wheel tables."

"Darb—"

Darb looks off, a whittled silhouette in the backseat. "Don't wanna know the details. I have no yen for gossip. Or polygamy. I respect the integrity of other folks' homesteads, unlike some people who I am tempted to slap in the back of the head."

"Just blasted limestone up there," Shaker says.

"Shitsky," Darb grumbles, racking his duffel's zipper. "Maybe a noogie or two at the next traffic signal would suffice."

Shaker ignores the road and peers past his own ashen reflection in the rearview mirror. Rather than pale, his cousin appears reddened, wind-lashed, abraded.

"Glad you're out," Shaker says.

"Out?"

"Prison."

"Oh, that. Had an overcrowding situation. They unleashed me the weekend before Turkey Day. I spent my holiday on a Greyhound aimed for Tuscaloosa, but I gave up somewheres in Kentucky. That woman." He trails off. "Kentucky is the pits."

"That was two months ago."

"You got yourself a calendar? That's good. Learn your presidential birthdays."

"My point—"

"A man need not explain his every furlough."

"I'll grant you that one."

"How fucking kind. Charity from a snowflake."

The anxious zippering ceases. Darb has removed a tin of cat food, peeled its aluminum seal, and begun to snack. "I seen the ugly crater where you used to have a house," he says while chewing.

"Bulldozed."

"Least they did a smooth job. When life hands you wrecking balls, etceteras. I mean, just look at you playing nursemaid to a hooker and her beautiful gimp. I am big with awe."

"Interpretive dancer," Shaker corrects him. "Of sorts."

Darb shrugs and licks the rim of his tin. "You found a way to navigate your confused affairs, good for you and your affairs. Me? I am maintaining. There is a straight road, and I intend to cling. Speaking of roads, you're about to run us off this one."

Shaker swerves. The vehicle resumes a safe channel in the single lane. Darb snickers in the backseat, reaches an arm up, and clamps it ruggedly on Shaker's shoulder.

"Us bozos," he says and squeezes.

But he doesn't ask the questions Shaker expects him to ask, not about the hazmat or the secluded landfill or the monument itself: rigged upright and unharmed, very complete, on account of Shaker perfecting the garbage-to-chicken-wire ratio. Also, all that Super Glue. Shaker's daily habit is to circle the monument like a disoriented animal, obsessively searching out cracks and crumbles and deficiencies in posture, pasting things. But today, he stands with Darb at the clearing's cusp, peering instead at his cousin. Darb and his red face are motionless. He's not even looking at the monument, Shaker realizes, not the whole length at least. Only the top, the crowning piece, the item de résistance. Mort's gasmask. Shaker has wondered for weeks if the mask was too sentimental, a dubious taste. But Darb doesn't object. He doesn't say anything. Instead, he wraps an arm around Shaker and taps his tongue on the ridge of his dentures. The sound inside him is clean, abrupt.

"That's classic," Darb says and climbs back in the car.

*

They are soberly carousing the streets on a breeze-flattened Monday evening. Darb has declined even an innocent prune-and-piss juice at the Beagle, insisting he wants to hold to his current teetotaler streak. Four months and thirteen days. He won't enter bars or stroll the beer aisle at the grocery mart or make sarcastic jabs about the sleek liquor advertisements pasted outside the local preschool. He says he passes up the fake wine in church, and the word *church* surprises Shaker. It sounds so fraught, so brittle in his cousin's mouth. Darb's mind is uncluttered, and Shaker has no argument here. So they drive. Sternly at first, but soon the old giddiness creeps in. Shaker honks the car horn at unsuspecting pedestrians. Each man has his window low and an arm out, finning the night air. Darb's seat is reclined to such an angle his kneecaps are level with his baldness. Shaker notes the Italian loafers on his cousin's feet. Imitations probably. The leisure suit makes Darb look like a giant, festering banana. Darb catches Shaker's expression and matches its vexation.

"That's a whole lot of yellow to drape on one man," Shaker says.

"Ain't it? I was standing at a bus depot in Pennsyltucky with my bag and my new haircut, looking at the departures board. And I really zeroed in on that word. Departures. It scared me to shit. Kinda obvious why. Then I turned around and saw a shoeshine gentleman in this outrageous suit, and I gave him all my money. Two hundred total. Now here I am, looking like a big, gay daffodil. It opens me up wide, the way my addictions used to. I am nude, an open target, ready before God. I dunno. That makes me feel more scrupulously loved."

"Both of us," Shaker says, "look like we're dressed for trick-or-treating."

Darb shifts against the upholstery in a fetal crouch and howls. The laughter is ribald, convulsive. The joke, Shaker thinks, was not so funny. It wasn't even a joke. The laughter disintegrates, and Darb uprights his seat with a long sigh. "They don't let you laugh like that on Trailways."

"I thought you took Greyhound."

"Pull over," he says.

"Here?"

"Pull over!" Darb shouts.

It's the shadier backend of Main Road. Porn shacks and tackle shops where the franchises have all failed. An ice cream truck, box-shaped and officiously white, is steel-booted alongside a fire hydrant, a wad of traffic citations tucked in the wiper blade. Marooned, it looks. The Frosty Brain Freeze and Sundae Bloody Sundae decals have been slandered with gangland graffiti. An outbreak of ivy rises up the grille. Darb gets out and walks between the two trucks, a pained blankness on his face. Something inside him is roiling. He looks to Shaker for an answer. Shaker shrugs.

Darb can't return his attention to the ice cream truck. He's squirming in his suit, plagued by some kind of unbearable itch, and that's how Shaker sees them. Across each wrist a recent, deliberate pink slash. Suicide souvenirs. Shaker looks up, looks away. Darb is still addressing him with the red bulb of his head, his features rabbled together. He stops grappling with himself. He sighs and buttons his coat. The scarred wrists slink back up his tacky sleeves.

"Just a *truck*," Darb says, as if stopping had been Shaker's idea all along.

Returned to their vehicle and carousing slower now, neither man speaks. The aimless patrol continues without incident. Darb asks to be dropped at his old apartment, and Shaker complies. He doesn't think to inquire whether his cousin is living there or not.

*

The woman is on the sofa in garters and nylons, leg slung over the arm ledge with crumpled dollars crammed into her dark pleats, as the hi-fi plays at a discreet volume. One of Shaker's ex-wife's feather boas lies athwart the coffee table. The ottoman holds a tiara. All the furniture, in fact, seems to be frozen in rival states of stupefaction, Shaker included. She scissors her legs wide and provides him an ample view. The most retort he can manage involves tensing his lips into a shrewd aperture, too small to speak. He's pretty sure the crumpled dollars are board game currency. The boa looks feral. Meanwhile, the stereo on the other side of the room isn't playing actual music, just soft tides of static. Shaker takes a step and his hazmat makes the most stupid-sounding crinkle. He tries to pause his breathing, attempt a tepid hello, but the woman snaps a garter. Shaker's internal machinery collapses in a pile of hooks and nails and crusted glue.

"Busy night?" she asks.

"Not until now."

"I wiggled across several miles of dirty stage, volcanic rubble, picnic tables, ocean floor. A few dozen men put their eyes inside me where their grubby fingers and gold bullion cannot reach. I starve myself without end or goal. I try to look my best. These are the dream songs of the sexually ineffectual."

"You want to fuck me by not fucking me."

"Not you. Everyone. Every*thing*. The mass is always more manageable than the poor, single, lonely soul at the other end of the telescope."

"I had a visitor today."

"I saw," she says. "I was only a few steps behind you with my cabbage aimed. I wanted to launch it at your head, cannonball style."

"That's sort of beautiful," Shaker whispers.

"Should I break out the blow darts?"

"He's harmless."

"I'm not," she spits.

"You're bored with the fiefdom."

"Come here and say that to my angry little—"

"Vagina," Shaker blurts. "Vagina, vagina, vagina."

He reaches out and steadies himself on a lava lamp that is providing most of the mood lighting for the current inquisition.

"You don't like my vamping. You don't like my death threats. What does a girl have to do to get a little mastery of the situation? And don't say penis hickeys."

Shaker lets go the lamp, looking at her, lightheaded and cross-eyed.

"Do something," he says.

"Me or you?"

"Either. Both. Garters optional."

"You survived so long without me."

"Stop."

"You pretended I didn't exist after I left."

"Don't."

"Tell me how much you missed me. How needy you became, how jaded, how dismal. Itemize all the wonderful ways I destroyed your life, and then sit back and relax and let me lick the gloom out of you like Oreo filling."

Shaker mumbles something barely audible, something unlike any English he's ever heard or tried to speak. Perhaps he's turned feral, too. And not only him. The woman is curled into a small nylon ball, writhing around under the lace and dangling hasps, as she rubs herself with a lackadaisical hand.

A distant voice, muffled in couch cushion, asks: "Is this real enough for you?"

But Shaker can't answer because he is already lunging against the sofa bolster where her ass is arched. After wrestling off the hazmat and stretching aside the panty silk, he inaugurates the lovemaking act with a bravado that seems utterly external to him. His face fills with stunned absorption, his vision blearily trained on the back of her downturned head. The room seems to pivot around them, as if on castors. She's rocking along to a languorous tempo that Shaker can't exactly locate. Every object and surface is glinting up at him warily. Shaker, the lucky stud, manages two and a half chivalrous thrusts before he clenches, stammers, coughs an apology, and prematurely leaks what feels like a gallon's worth of his genetic soup down her backside. She moans and pushes her cold bottom against him, her flesh goose-pimpled, rose-blotched. Without realizing it, Shaker has already detached. He palms his face, sweeps back his greasy bangs, and glances helplessly around the room, hoping to regain armature, any armature. Mostly, he tries not to feel so glum about the milky dribble that has gathered in the grooves of the couch's crimped upholstery.

"Are those mutton chops absolutely necessary?" she asks over her shoulder.

"Huh?"

"The things on your face. Your sideburns."

"Right," he replies, touching them with an exploratory thumb. "Those."

He shakes off his undershirt and hands it to her. Rather than wipe her thighs, she snuggles the fabric to her face, whiffing deeply.

"Is that how it always was with her?"

"More or less," Shaker says, bashful, still chugging breath. "Usually less."

The woman flattens herself upon the couch's contoured leather.

"I bet she doesn't even know," she says, dropping the item of clothing and reaching back to grab the muscle flab on his leg, squeezing and releasing this, too. "Now please don't touch me ever again."

*

Days after, while shoveling the snow that has drifted up the driveway in waves, like rolls of frozen surf, Shaker entertains the prospect of inviting Darb and his garish suit to come live at Agog Manor. He fantasizes about the cousins bunking beds, sharing dental floss, donning matching jammies, glomming onto each other like old times. One more husband for the woman to rehearse her precarious wifery upon. But Darb could already be gone, too, seated on another interstate bus bound for Tuscaloosa, Florida, Bowling Green. Shaker has his qualms. He only wants to keep at his work. The shoveling and salting duties occupy his body in a way that assuages as much as it exhausts. His attention is directed in troughs and vectors and distinct points. The Tullys soon arrive with fresh chains on their tires and a new task. A popular youth center has turned inferno. Shaker rides hump in silence, a respectful passenger, cautiously chewing the crusted chap off his lip.

There isn't much youth center left. The rumpus mats and alphabet blocks and lending library are melted into the snow, splotchy colorful stains that look like poker chips scattered from afar. Shaker sweeps it all into a pile with his foot while the Brothers pick clean the only surviving artifacts. Hamster wheel. Hamster hammock. Hamster condominium with aboveground hamster pool. The hamsters and their swank habitats are going to outlast us all, Shaker thinks, and for the first time in weeks he feels halfway hopeful.

The men bucket the rainbow silt and drive to their landfill. The sky has started snowing again, loosely. The stray flakes feel moist upon Shaker's forehead as he stands in the shadow of his monument, gazing upwards, realizing after several minutes' consideration that the monument is intact, perfectly preserved in this long and dreary weather, but Mort's gasmask is missing.

14.

Most days, Shaker finds the woman in the kitchen, where she has hauled along most of the garage. Broken guitars, shattered maracas, an old Fender Tweed ripped apart, mid-autopsy. All this equipment she has begun to clinically dismantle in knots and sections and curly strands. Shaker observes the massacre from the breakfast nook, a UN peacekeeper keeping uneasy watch over a war-trounced and blood-caked land, afraid of criticizing the local voodoo. Royce has been wheeled to the window with a look of utmost blissfulness. The recorded yodeling has paused. An electric accordion is disemboweled across the counter, and the woman loosens its mechanical guts from the steel box frame. She digs her free arm back into the amp. She's been at this horror show for hours.

"This mean you've killed the bluegrass, too?" Shaker asks.

"You'd like that."

"Royce agrees with me."

"I have a process," she says. "A whole theoretical scaffolding, and a scaffolding for that scaffolding. You're too much a prude to try to understand it. Any of it."

"I woke this morning to the sound of slave spirituals and sea shanties."

Ohms, amperage, voltage, impedance, whatever she's trying to undo, she drops it in a pile.

"Selfhood is the ultimate tyranny, the ultimate oppression. You need to break it apart to see the bigger patterns at play. Destruction, then doubt. Mystery, then pilgrimage. Eventually, that leads to rebirth. That's the whole cycle, the chain."

"You're regressing," Shaker says.

"She ventured forth into noise and abstraction and the avant-garde? I'm working my way backwards through the influences and rudiments, seeking the original source, the source of *her*. And that starts with the end of all this, this, this...material."

Shaker hoists his beverage cooler.

"You're taking Royce on a picnic," she says.

"Just myself. He looks so happy there at the window, now that the Viking throat-singing has been eradicated."

"You think my work is silly. Silly and sad and relentlessly pathetic."

"Some ancient cultures believe that accordion is an aphrodisiac," Shaker says, edging up beside her.

"Oh yeah? Well, I heard the best singers in the world are castratos. Where's my knife?"

She lifts the steel box into the crook of her arm and taps its keys. The chord is fumbled and ugly, but Shaker can hear it. A wheezing, medieval sound.

Shaker trudges off toward the garage, nervously adjusting the crotch of his pants.

*

Triple-stack pb&j sandwich, pecan cookies with brown sugar glaze, coffee in thermos, two cans of cat food. The cooler is packed. Shaker has even brought along a portable space heater from the basement, plus a hundred feet of extension cord, in case his cousin is living in a teepee or ice-fishing shack. But Darb isn't outside his old apartment as Shaker had assumed. No recreational campers or indigenous refugees in tents, no displaced bachelors hibernating on the yard. The yard is empty. Shaker heads for Darb's disaster site and doesn't find a tent or shack, either, only the thing. Shaker isn't sure what else to call it. He thinks of it only as *the thing*, a manifest presence, the same way a sunblind beachgoer looks across the Atlantic Ocean and muddily announces: *France.*

The structure sits just beyond the house's blackened foundation, a semi-sphere shape twenty feet across and only partway built, nude frame. The exoskeleton of an igloo? Bio-dome greenhouse? Latticed mushroom cap? Shaker can't tell if the thing is a shelter or obstruction or standalone art piece. Is his cousin sleeping in that?

Shaker nears the structure with a slow-footed gait, his hands in his pockets and a fake smile seared into his face. Darb is still wearing the daffodil suit. His head is hidden inside a welder's mask, and he's taking a blowtorch to the structure's crisscrossed beams and gaps, all jointed into mass. The thing needs reinforcing, Shaker knows. There are snowdrifts to contend with, vain gravities, heavy weathers. He stands beside Darb, nodding his head rotely, his tongue a strained scrap of muscle folded neat inside his mouth.

"Work in progress," Darb says and snuffs the torch. "The base was a bitch-and-a-half, but that is what happens when you forsake blueprints and go at a vision freehand."

"Looks like a...a..." Shaker is low on the ground, peering upward, trying to find a revelatory angle. He stands and scratches his head.

"Geodesic dome," explains Darb.

"Okay," Shaker says. "I don't know what that is."

"Just what it seems like."

"Aluminized Swiss cheese?"

"Yeah, that's a funny comparison."

"There is a distinct odor."

"I learned about them from Mort. Details are still a mite sketchy, but the dome's the real dream. Had to make it a sensible scale, of course."

"It's the metalwork," Shaker says, sniffing. "The material."

"Cat food tins. I melt them and weld them. My recyclables."

He indicates the abundance of trash bags heaped in a pyramid beside the backup propane tank, the tape measure and yardstick, a wrench collection outspread in the snow. Shaker recognizes the wrenches as his own but doesn't mention it.

"You can never have too many monuments, I guess."

"He was my boy," Darb replies stiffly.

He resets his jaw, dentures aligned, and resumes the blowtorch. "Still deciding the best way to present it for public viewing. If it needs some kind of backdrop or maybe a spotlight or type of gala. A geodesic dome, people usually go gaga for the spectacle."

Shaker doesn't mention the missing mask, either. He doesn't offer a sandwich nibble, or nip of lukewarm coffee, or the heat packets he brought in bulk. Instead, he clears his throat and gets a good, strong voice going. "Ya know what? I should probably head home. My autoharp needs a vasectomy."

*

The problem is Shaker did better work than he thought. The monument's summit is several layers of drywall long-screwed into a masonry of enamel and aluminum and pyrite and plank, all cauterized like a wound and buttressed with surplus wire. He has to hack apart the stack with a canoe oar. With pliers, he peels away the chicken wire and employs a saber saw to decapitate the monument peak, which he tarps and sets aside for future use like the top tier of a wedding cake. Then he begins his usual build, keenly aware he previously scavenged the best articles. And so Shaker finds himself groveling around subzero February with shovel and hammer, prying loose sloughed polymer wherever he can find it. He thinks of childhood stories that involved buried riches and the rollicking escapades of lone men on desert islands, eccentric pensioners and beachcombers with metal detectors, all castaways of some sort. Shaker is not sure where he fits in the lineage, if he has some alternate pedigree, or maybe no pedigree at all. He continues until dusk and somehow manages to add sixteen inches to the spine. Because any additional height also requires additional width, Shaker starts pulling off more and more chicken wire, slow and then recklessly, causing fifteen and a half erect feet of alloyed trash to come toppling down on him, pinning his limbs to a small parcel of petrified landfill for the next thirty-six hours.

*

When the Tullys stumble across him, Shaker has turned an unsavory blue color and is subsisting on a single rationed cookie that his teeth are too numb to chew. He's basically just sucking the glaze for sustenance. Trapped under six hundred pounds of crumbled monument, his blood circulation continues unabated thanks to the disposable heat packets that line his parka. Shaker has only to repeatedly punch himself in the chest to activate their warmth. The cold-induced dementia has added several coats of permafrost to his brain, a brain that can now only communicate with itself in crude burps and jumbled lullabies. The space heater never made it out of the car. The heat packets are burning him severely. Shaker's self-pugilism may have fractured a rib.

The Tullys approach the accident scene with their arms full of sacked dross they came to deploy. They arch over Shaker, scanning him for any last twinklings of life.

"I think I see France," Shaker tells them before lapsing into a calm and restful coma.

*

Shaker wakes in bed under an avalanche of steaming towels. A Tully sits on each side of him, and a woman who resembles his ex-wife is warming his toe knuckles with a curling iron. Her handsome stroke-victim husband sits in a wheelchair at the window, making soft swishing sounds with his lips. Royce seems to be on the brink of imparting some vital intelligence that Shaker is not yet ready to hear. Shaker tries to sit up, but the hot towels scald him. The notches in his spine are fused together, one stolid slab. He relaxes under the weight of all this mollycoddled recovery and remarks to the Tully on his left, "My cauliflower is burning."

"Oh god," the woman moans. "I don't think I can handle another vegetable at the breakfast table."

"Breakfast," Shaker says. "Sounds lovely."

"Stay still."

"An act of sabotage," he tells them. "I saw it in a vision. Somebody loosened the rivets on my stump. My stack."

"I understand that he has always been a little drug-damaged," she says. "But will the idiot live?"

The Tullys stare at Shaker, then nod at each other and nod at the woman, who returns the nod and presses the curling iron against the tender undersides of Shaker's feet. The room fills with the smell of barbecued flesh. Shaker yelps and she unplugs the torture device.

"That's better," she says and walks out.

Shaker is adapting nicely to the hot towels that wrap his throat, his torso, his arms. The Tullys, for their part, stare past the roasting cocoon to the small parts of land-fill slag that Shaker hugged all the way into this bed.

"Bury me with it," says Shaker.

The Tullys sigh and depart the room. Shaker is alone with Royce, and Royce is snoring beatifically in his chair.

Springtime is almost upon them.

*

But it's another month before the warmness returns to the corn-belt latitudes. By that point, Shaker is prepared. The chargrilled patches on his feet have healed. He's plucked his overgrown eyebrows, expunged the lint from his navel, and filed his canine fangs down to inoffensive nubs.

"The good news is I got my old machine back," he tells her. "Part-time. Afternoons only. Once again, I am riding the Waring blender. I should still be available to take Royce to his tap dance lessons."

Shaker can't read the woman's reaction. She has a pair of swim goggles stretched around the top half of her face and a red-checker bandanna curtaining the rest. The kitchen has been transformed by a moody chiaroscuro of dark smoke and skewed lighting, her experimental destruction having expanded to include all the plumbing and cabinetry and electric in the walls. She stands amid the puddled water and broken pipes, scrutinizing the tendril of torn cable in her hand, shaking her head dismissively. Shaker steps forward and tries to repeat his sentence, realizing too late that her ears are plugged, too. She hasn't been listening to him at all.

She hasn't been wearing much clothing, either, not while she conducts this domestic mayhem, no makeup or jewelry or psychedelic skin paint. Just an ordinary nude body balkanized by uneven tan lines and cellulite dents. Shaker wants to avoid leering, although he respectfully notes she has continued to groom her pubic region into delightful topiary patterns. Once he's recovered the sensation in his nerves, he undertakes an adolescent odyssey of rampant self-abuse in all the unused and undemolished rooms of the manor. In this way, he steels his resolve and continues to concentrate on his own ludicrous project. He has secretly mailed the town planning board about zoning and height variances but received no response.

Springtime brings the usual up-tick in combustions. The Tullys are making daily deposits at the landfill, bringing so much exploded wreckage that Shaker benefits from all sorts of novel finds. He upgrades wire brands, epoxies, a more aerodynamic selection of trash. He finds a few more arrowheads and involves them in the construction. A rim of refuse now borders the flat range, blockading it from the natural elements. Shaker is slowly starting to understand the location suffers from rotten drainage, so he rigs a sump-pump around the monument's base that ultimately malfunctions and nourishes a bloated moat. He fashions a canopy of patio parasols above an antique wicker chair to keep Royce cool and dry in case the gray gentleman is ever again smuggled back to the site. Here Shaker sometimes sits with an Instamatic camera, documenting the monument's new expansion. Twenty-five feet tall. He thinks he can reach forty. The photographs he stashes under his cot at home, like some shameful clump of sticky porno pages. He tells the woman he's thinking of growing a beard to go with all the new hair on his palms.

*

They continue to come humping over the hills, a dozen homeless men in their rag tatters and trash sack ponchos, heads hooded, only the grayness of their gray hands and gray chins and gray chin stubble protruding. From Shaker's high angle, it almost appears they have risen intact from the garbage acreage itself. Nearer and nearer, they sway as they walk, a martial formation that somehow moves across the rough terrain without the tentative stepping and clumsy footholds that signal even a seasoned rubbish-strider like Shaker. He pauses his chainsaw, which he had been using to symmetrize the northwest corner after he accidentally took off too much on the opposite side. He dismounts the ladder and waits for them to clear the garbage barrier, the homeless men swaying and walking and swaying, a circle around his circle. Shaker is almost hypnotized by the procession. He shoulders the chainsaw with a rope sling and uses a deformed pool ladle to pole-vault himself over the moat, overshoots his mark, and crashes into a pair of men at the end of their train. The men go down, rise immediately, and continue their slow trek. Shaker has difficulty getting to his feet, burdened as he is with the chainsaw on his shoulder and a second and third chainsaw tied to each leg.

"Beautiful day!" he shouts after them. "I took my dog for a walk this morning! Sunshine out the goddamn wazoo!"

The rain continues to come down on him in razors and clots.

*

The bones of the manor seem to be shifting around in congress with the clamor. Up in the third-floor attic, Shaker is idly harvesting pieces of insulation fluff from the walls, a superior brand of firing-range earmuffs clamped on his head. But he can still feel the breakage downstairs, which has achieved a kind of steady tribal rhythm. THUMP, thump, thump, thump, THUMP, thump, thump, thump. The woman has abandoned medieval nostalgia for the Paleolithic period. These must be the primal stirrings of early earth, Shaker thinks, a music forged in mountain caverns and desolate plains, drummed on tanned skins, splintered skulls. Although that does not explain the wailing smoke alarm. Royce is dressed in Shaker's hazmat, his head turbaned with a towel, shins and wrists strapped to his wheelchair so the vibrations do not spill him. Shaker makes sure the fastenings are still secure, and then he wends his way downstairs, carefully avoiding the ruck of fallen sheet-rock and broken plaster and twisted pipe, a cat's cradle of black cables disgorged from a ceiling tile.

She is sitting inside a circle of candles with her legs folded, a sledgehammer in her lap. A pagan meditation of sorts. The walls around her are punctured with dozens and dozens of holes.

"I thought I heard the mailman screaming for help," Shaker says.

With his pajama strings clutched in a fist, he shoots back up the stairs.

*

The backyard, at least, offers a small oasis of calm. She looks pensive beside the bonfire, her head tilted, the smoke draining up to the night sky. She holds a garden trowel and stabs the air without rhythm. If there is some secret cadence hidden inside the bonfire's crackles and sizzles and snaps, Shaker cannot hear it. Inside the burning barrel are unspooled reels, tapes, vivisectioned instruments, amplifier parts. All of it crumpled and wilting under the expanding flames. A lone tentacle, black-charred, hangs over the side in a half-swoop. Shaker steps back and fans the smoke fumes from his face, tuning into the monologue already in progress.

"Everyone laughs at her now. Once she started making songs with animal sounds, air raid sirens, Cuisinarts. Once she started hiring body doubles to make unsanctioned appearances at children's birthday parties and wedding anniversaries and job fairs, a hundred pale imitations of her haunting public spaces and city parks. Everyone is so bloody literal these days. No imagination, no gusto or verve. Humans are conditions. They molt like conditions. Transmogrify. How else to capture the whole burly tantrum of existence?"

Shaker shrugs.

"You pretend not to care," she tells him.

"Doesn't interest me."

"Liar."

"That doesn't interest me, either," Shaker says.

"You look back, you dwell. You're just as much a stooge for nostalgia as everyone else. The problem with most people is they can't bear the bizarre and new, and they can't bear the final pangs of anything. So nostalgia is that sweet spot, a way of hiding in the cozy past. An eternal return."

"You're really not gonna use any of this junk? Because if you're not—"

"She's becoming more obscure, more of a joke, a ghost of a ghost." The woman drops the trowel into the fire, removes the goggles, and stares egg-eyed at Shaker. "She is becoming more and more like me."

"You're missing the appendectomy scar," he says. "The chicken pox blemishes. A bong burn on her inner thigh."

"Superficialities. She and I are standing on opposite sides of the same void. She moved forward into noise, strangeness, the future, the unknown? I'm retreating backwards into the long, gray dark of history, where nostalgia can't reach. And maybe we'll meet somewhere in the middle."

Shaker has so far successfully avoided rubbernecking at her nudeness. But as she narrows her eyes on him, he looks away, looks down, sees the flesh, and settles upon it. He ogles until his vision burns against the smoke.

"It's only sausage casing," she says. "No different than yours, hers, anyone's."

Shaker sleeves the sweat from his forehead, the heat on his face, the tingles of hellfire under and outside and within.

"You'd like to devour me right here," she says. "Lay me down and ball me in the twilight of our pot greenhouse. Or maybe ravish me in the backseat of that hideous SUV atop Royce's hemorrhoid cushion. Is that it? Is that all? Some lame bourgeois sex fantasy from the softcore channel?"

"There's a whole channel for that?"

"Fantasies are just nightmares that have yet to curdle."

"I need...ice," he stutters. "Frozen ice."

"How many times?"

"Wha?"

"Before the fantasy gets dull, disappears. How long until we wear the whole lust out? Stop counting on your fingers!"

Shaker makes an arrogant scoffing sound, then tries to inconspicuously hide the hand behind his back. She steps closer, still engrossed.

"But a thing that never happens? That not-happening is forever," she says, dropping her goggles in the fire. "You can't kill that. It never dies. Isn't that beautiful?"

"It already happened. The garters, the couch."

"I remember no such thing," she replies. "I am a happily married woman who respects the sanctity of her marriage bed and has hydrochloric acid oozing from her slot."

Shaker returns his concentration to the pyre, the magnetic tape and instrument pieces and strings twisting up in the blaze, like flora in time-lapse photography, a rapid magic. It makes him breathless with exhilaration and dread as all that viney material blackens and shrinks and is gone.

*

The vantage is not great. Shaker was able to glean more information from the morning newspaper, a front-page article that detailed a local father's struggle to redeem his dead son's reputation with a little-understood art project and the corporate sponsorship that is aiding his cause. Mother Clucker's Fried Chicken & Sandwich Takeout is collecting donated cat food cans from three separate counties. There are daily autograph hounds, an audience of spectators. A TV truck parked behind the dome has sprouted an impressive assortment of radar dishes like fungi. From where he is crouched in a ditch across the road, Shaker cannot decipher the restaurant banner sagging like an empty turtleneck between fence posts. He inches forward, but an overcrowded sedan has slowed on the road. They honk their horn until Darb pauses his welding and gives them a distracted wave. The car drives off. Darb, way up in the sky and precariously tottering on his forty-foot stepladder, shakes his head with annoyance and re-lights his torch.

15.

The Howitzer positions himself a polite distance upwind, arms folded, face blank, tipping the tremendous architecture of his bald head. This seems an endorsement of sorts, although Shaker isn't reassured. Behind the men, Royce has his nose dappled with lotion like a beach lifeguard while he gets sunbaked into his chair. The Howitzer shifts his gaze from monument to invalid to monument again. Shaker does not seem to factor much into the panorama. He has measured the monument at thirty-three feet, although that number doesn't account for wind erosion or the temperature swells and shrinkage that are beyond Shaker's management. Thirty-three feet: one for every year of Christ's life. That detail feels significant, even to a godless trash-hugger like Shaker. He knows how easily it could happen. Hammering in the dark one night, a quick sneeze, a missed swing, the nail driven through his palm. Shaker isn't sure what's more appalling, the pretention of self-crucifixion or the homeless men poaching his shoes. The homeless men are scarce today. Shaker sidles up against the Howitzer, trying to hold himself in league, smelling only his own mildew, none from the trash.

"Apples to oranges," the Howitzer says.

"The Patriot-Tribune told me they'd send a reporter over. That was a week ago. Then today, they put another picture of him on the front page. Some yokel wrote a letter to the editor suggesting they enter the damn thing into the National Register of Historic Places. Declare it a landmark. An art critic from Toledo said it looks like an explosion of flamingo legs in a lawn ornament factory. That was a *compliment*. I'm nowhere near finished, and he's just tinkering for kicks. I fear I'm being routed."

"Who's the vegetable?"

"My lucky rabbit's foot, Royce."

"I think Royce is getting too much sun."

"He's from California. They all look summer-stunned on the western coast. I had some patio umbrellas for him, but I had to repurpose them."

"Shaker," says the Howitzer, "I don't know what I'm doing out here."

"Me neither," Shaker replies, resting a foot on Royce's wicker chair. "I'm being routed, aren't I?"

"Yes," the Howitzer says.

"It's a round world. People like round things."

"And they don't like traipsing around garbage dumps, either."

"An oversight," Shaker agrees.

"Plus, he's got the better arc. Failure, exile, redemption. Total package."

"You see yesterday's editorial?"

"Stop reading the newspaper, Shaker."

"There's talk of a ribbon-cutting ceremony, a posthumous pardon." Shaker shakes his head.

"The one thing that baffles me," the Howitzer says, "is why he painted the whole thing pink. Crazy fucker."

"The pardon part I'm okay with."

"Sure."

"I'm being routed to hell."

"What I see is an issue of stability."

Shaker points to the top of the monument, far up there, thirty-three feet of wavering stack. "It used to have a topper."

"Not what I mean."

"I know what you mean," Shaker mutters.

"The people I sometimes work for. My odd soldier-of-fortune jobs. They have not forgotten you."

Shaker cracks a knuckle. "Tell them I already got someone busting apart my kitchen. Although I guess it's not my kitchen."

"The Tullys owe them, too. It's all one big shadiness."

"Guessing these people also got you for some pointless debt."

The Howitzer is absently fingering the lanyard of keys around his stallion neck and is about to speak when Shaker cuts him off:

"The explosion at his house. Maybe it wasn't a freak accident. Maybe the blowfish lab didn't blow up. Maybe it was arson. An insurance scam. Maybe he just wanted some sympathy, some attention."

"You think your cousin exploded his own house on purpose, killed his own boy."

"Some people can't help themselves," Shaker replies. "They find a decent thing to love and it loves them back, and they aren't satisfied until they scuttle it."

The Howitzer has approached the monument and pried free a small piece. He holds it up and hikes an eyebrow. An empty can of spray paint. Flamingo pink. Shaker's face burns a similar hot shade, and he tries to look away.

The Howitzer takes him gently by the chin and trains Shaker's head on the peak of the monument, the middle, the base.

"Bulldoze it," says the Howitzer.

Then, just as gently, he releases Shaker and turns his attentions to Royce, reapplying the suntan lotion in even streaks until the cream is invisible and Royce's face is a cheerful, gleaming slice of gray meat.

"Let's go for a drive," the Howitzer says.

*

The truck cab is at capacity. Shaker had earlier filled the backseat with a trove of malevolent tools—hacksaws, chainsaws, table saws, etc.—that he now refuses to explain or condone. Instead, he rides shotgun, ruefully watching the rearview. Royce is secured on the truck bed with forty feet of bungee and two rolls of gaffer tape, solidly affixed, and still the Howitzer insists on driving half the speed limit. Royce seems enthralled with his roofless journey. His tastefully manicured haircut explodes in a frizzy corona. A nascent sunburn is starting to pinken his cheeks. The Howitzer drives so slow their twenty-mile trek across town takes more than an hour to complete.

They eventually arrive at an old garbage dump that has not seen consistent use in years, maybe decades.

"I had no idea this place existed," Shaker says.

"You sure about that, chief?"

Shaker makes a noncommittal throat noise. He fusses with a broken latch on the glovebox, not removing his seatbelt yet.

"Should we, uh, untape and unbungee our human payload?" he asks.

"Don't worry about Mr. Royce," the Howitzer replies, reaching over and unbuckling Shaker's seatbelt for him. "This won't take long."

They step out of the truck and stride up and over the first hill, and that's when Shaker sees them, all of them.

"Oh, come on," he mumbles.

Before him is a wide, gray field full of half-built trash stumps, several dozen, all moldering and atilt, long abandoned. Shaker cautiously descends the slope and tiptoes among the rows. He studies and prods with a gnarled TV aerial he has found on the ground. The Howitzer follows behind him, mirthlessly sucking a lollipop. He stops when Shaker stops. He sighs when Shaker sighs.

The tallest stump barely reaches Shaker's chest, and he stabs it with the aerial repeatedly, unproductively.

"You don't remember building them, do you."

Shaker shakes his head, too dumbstruck to speak.

"Two or three years ago," the Howitzer says. "It was quite the crime spree. You ransacked people's cars, stole their furniture, knocked parts off their houses. I guess the regular garbage here wasn't good enough material. Sound familiar?"

"None of it."

"Now do you understand why so many folks in our lovely community loathe you? Why a certain select group of citizens would so gleefully fuck with your life?"

Shaker faces the Howitzer with a wounded look, innocent and pale.

"Not really," he says and walks back to the truck, the aerial tucked under his arm, nabbing a few additional trash items along the way.

*

The usual smorgasbord mess on the kitchen table— decimated foodstuffs and cannibalized musical equipment—has been replaced. The LP sleeve is stark black. There are no names or song titles or production credits, no identifiable features of any kind. Shaker flips the LP over, peers inside the cracked shrink-wrap, grimacing.

"Is this it?" he asks.

"You know it is."

"Welp, I guess your big payday has arrived."

"Turns out the whole record label lawsuit thing was a publicity stunt. That rich husband of hers owns the company. They were just trying to drum up interest. Doesn't matter. It was worth the wait."

"What's this one? Banshee wails? Undersea implosions? Pet sounds?"

"There's no sound at all. Total silence."

"Silence," Shaker nods.

"It's 87 minutes long. Three movements. 19 tracks. It's a *double* album. And not a single note of music anywhere on it. I've already listened to it twice. It's her rawest, most honest creation yet."

"So it's another publicity stunt."

"I think it's genius."

There is an overfull accordion file on the floor. Hundreds of Post-it notes, index cards, random scraps are tacked around the room, months of meticulous scribblings. Shaker is more interested in her solder gun. He picks it up and swings it by its cord. He twirls it on his finger, sharpshooter style, while sucking his under lip in concentration. He's wondering how in all his blundering, sticky addictions he never once managed to glue his nostrils shut.

"You're not listening," she says.

"Nope."

"She's moved beyond songs, beyond sound. Not noise, but white noise. Layers and layers of holy reverential quiet. The Final American Pause." Her face glazes together, a sheen of panic. "How am I ever going to recreate that?"

The woman snatches back the tool before he can accidentally set his garments aflame and tosses it in the trash. Shaker sulks off. Passing through the foyer, he catches sight of his own face in the windowpane. Loose jawed, hooded eyes. Classic mouthbreather in repose. Then Shaker seizes up, realizing he's not the mouthbreather.

Darb is on the front stoop with his face crushed against the frosted glass. He has a bouquet of plastic bags—all empty—puckered in his armpit. Seeing Shaker, he blinks a few times and begins to jam on the doorbell, frowning bleakly. Shaker cautiously opens the door to the width of his head. Darb gives the bell a final stab, still peering into the window's opaqueness. Shaker coughs, taps the glass, and gets a glimpse of his cousin's unfrosted eyes. Small balls marbled with bloodshot.

"Cousin," Darb says. "The glass in this house don't even look like glass."

"Strange, that."

"I'm out here getting stalked by paparazzo."

Shaker is nodding. He contracts his jowls, reshapes his face. Into what, precisely, he has no idea. "Good for you."

Darb gives the doorbell another ring.

"Stop that," Shaker says.

"I always wanted to live an awe- and grandeur-filled life, but these days I'm just happy to wake up without my sex organ in a sling. One nut always hangs a little lower than the other. Just splenetic, I guess. I'm a whole glossary of hinky vibes. My gum lines hurt. Somebody cheer me up."

"You need a carnival."

"I do," Darb says, forcing a grin. The corrugated wrinkles of his forehead are limned with sweat. "And groceries."

"All that donated cat food is gone?"

Darb looks off down the cul-de-sac. "These den moms and snide Eagle Scouts and town council douches are still bringing me supplies for the dome. Tools and light setups and endorsement deals. All the tins are *empty.* I haven't eaten anything for days." He puts away the hand and shrugs. "I got nobody to drive me for my groceries."

*

The road paver is a one-seat machine with a spindly woman riding atop in an orange hardhat and vest, rolling along slowly, straightening the parking lot's fresh tar while Shaker watches, rapt, from the condiment aisle. All that stretched open surface. He doesn't know why, but the sight depresses him. Darb snaps his fingers, and the reverie is broken. He is asking for the basket. Shaker trots over with the basket raised. His cousin pitches in the mesquite sauce and cayenne pepper and two spatulas, then moves into the taco department. Shaker follows, occasionally glancing outside at the empty lot and the paver slugging its black path to nowhere.

Darb finds his guacamole and hot sauce, his fruit preserves and instant frosting, and he passes a whipped cream display without a second look, instead pillaging a nearby shelf of all its peanut butter and maple syrup. The basket is full, so Shaker grabs another. Darb fills this with a dozen different kinds of pasta sauce. Extra Chunky. Thousand Vegetable. International Cheese. Every variety but the creamy vodka brand. Darb doubles back and does a second pass of the salad dressings and oils, and he guides Shaker to the checkout station. The men are waiting in their short line, pretending not to notice the tabloid racks, when Shaker says, "Any food?"

"Huh?"

"Food." Shaker pats the condiments rolling towards the barcode reader. The cashier is a sunny retiree, swiping each item under the red laser like a piece of flypaper

183

he's trying to shake off his hand. "These are only garnishes."

"So?" Darb asks.

"Never mind."

"We can score the cat food later," Darb explains, his red face growing redder. "It ain't going anywhere."

The elderly cashier is halfway through the inventory before he looks up and greets them. Darb is bent down, muzzily searching the candy case in their aisle. He grabs a chocolate bar and slams it on the conveyor belt, jolting the rubber off its track. The cashier apologizes and rings for his supervisor. Darb tries to speak, but he is sobbing too hard, gut-punched by some swift and inexplicable grief.

The cashier tries to marshal the chubby skin of his face into something that resembles a smile. "Any coupons today?"

But Darb is weeping hysterically, humpbacked, janking his arms. Shaker digs around his pockets to find a tissue or hanky. But all he has on his person are two solder guns filched from the manor, plus his halitosis and a dire case of dry scalp.

The old man swipes them through with such urgency he fails to ring up a few jars of baby food. Shaker pays with cash that he also filched from the manor and includes an ample tip. Then he hurriedly shoves Darb and Darb's overloaded baskets out the mechanical doors. Once they reach the parking lot, Shaker looks back and sees the cashier in animated conversation with the teenage manager. Shaker is trying to read their lips when he's pegged in the snout with a packet of dairy creamer.

"I love you, cousin. More than I love these fucking snacks. You know that, right?"

Darb is squinting through the tears and slush, holding a handful of packets, winding up for another throw. This one Shaker dodges with a skillful pirouette. The next packet grazes Shaker's cheek. Darb dumps the armload and goes for the baby food.

"The glass—" Shaker says.

The carrot-cream goulash explodes at Shaker's feet. Shaker takes a big step to avoid the shatter, tripping over his bootlaces, and lands with a fartish smack.

Darb breaks a few more jars and asks, "Truce?" while leaning over Shaker with a bottle of salad dressing in each fist, several saliva bubbles bursting on his lips.

Shaker thinks it over.

"Nah," he replies and gets to his feet. The fresh pavement is sticky with colorful pastes, spurts, abstract arcs, crumbed glass.

"Already had most of this stuff at the camp anyway," Darb shrugs, cellophane crunching under his knockoff Italian loafers. "Really, I just wanted the quality time."

He walks off into traffic without his groceries, leaving a trail of gummy footprints behind him and Shaker standing there, still nodding, wondering where all the pavers of the republic get parked at night.

*

Maybe it is the sunlit morning or the songbirds refusing to surrender their station in the trees, or the sight of Royce chewing his cold leftover manicotti with an air of benediction, but the dark mood lifts. Shaker stops by the bakery for two dozen bagels and a sampler cup of cream cheese. He also buys a round of iced coffees, which the counter girl wedges into a polystyrene tray that Shaker giddily carries out to the truck, palm-up, like a trained waiter. It is almost nine o'clock. The miniature metropolis of warehouses and storage sheds, aluminum rooftops and rusted facades, has filled with workers and cars. Shaker parks the truck on the grassy shoulder of the maintenance road and carries the boxed bagels and coffee tray to the shed where his former coworkers are divvying up their equipment and holstering tools in belts. Shaker sees the tarp that hugs the bulky shape of his old machine. He tries to bravely ignore the wistful thaw in his chest. Hob is on a foldable chair, fastening bike clips to his pant cuffs. Before Shaker can reach him, he's blocked by an arm and almost spills breakfast.

"Back from the dead," says Thin, his gaunt features thrust up in Shaker's face. The man has lost teeth and hair, and his skull bone structure is more pronounced. His eyeballs, jittery and rodentesque, are shaking in the arctic caves of their sockets.

"Temporarily," Shaker says.

"You found better work."

"A benefactor. A patron saint. Probably temporary, too."

"This winter was a long one."

"Yes," Shaker replies.

"At least you had a royal palace to hole up in."

Even though he amounts to little more than a semi-verbal cadaver, Thin still manages to block the alley path. A few icy drips of coffee bead down Shaker's wrist.

"We seen you in that neighborhood," Thin hisses. "Don't get fucking caught or you'll ruin it for the rest of us. Land of the free and the freeloader and so on."

Shaker adjusts his hold on the tray, only growing heavier in his one arm.

Thin blows a breeze of coffin breath. "Some pals of ours had a party. Brown-and-cream-type castle. A real rager, man. Things got crazy in a sad, sad way. A Good

Samaritan came along and cleaned that party mostly up. Unfortunately, we are left to wonder about his intentions and why he still left a lot of fucking evidence just sorta lying around. Evidence that sits there to this day 'cause certain parties cannot exactly waltz back in there with fancy schmancy hazmats and a kooky whore who wears a wig."

Shaker winces at the man's egregious mouth decay. He isn't sure if he should nod or not nod, so he makes a confused compromise and tries neither, both.

"Maybe that party is ready to get started again," Thin smiles and steps aside, "now that our pal Shaky is on the neighborhood watch."

Hob is seated on the flatbed, hooking a new mulch bag on the mower. His goatee has been pruned into a handlebar arch that makes his lips seem smaller, bedeviled. He finishes securing the bag and tilts his mirror sunglasses so that he can stare down the bridge of his knurly nose, Shaker in the crosshairs.

"Breakfast?" Shaker sidearms a bagel at Hob.

With a deft wrist flick, Hob swats the food to the ground. "Dude, you don't even work here! I rehired your shabby ass, and you never showed up!"

"Been busy," Shaker says. "Charity work."

"So this is your idea of amends?"

"I don't think so."

"You are a fucking prick," Hob says.

"Don't you miss the banter?"

"I do not."

"I'm not really big on the amends scene."

"Yeah, no shit."

"I don't really like bagels, either," Shaker says, staring down at his stupid tray. He grabs another and lobs it at the wall of the tin shack, where it sticks in place, an unsightly furuncle, baked fresh and already rotting.

On the drive home, he sees her standing on the roadside of the industrial park. She's dressed in a familiar skirt, scrimpy and immodest, a baggy cutoff tank top that exhibits a lot of midriff, her augmentations. Shaker, a little wracked, stops near the corner. At a distance, he watches her hop from truck to truck. The drivers all display the same vacant look, mechanical and bored, as she tucks the money away and ties up her lush piles of possibly fake hair.

Maybe she's just selling them some greenhouse contraband, he tells himself, speeding away.

*

Shaker has to triple-check the address on the mailbox to confirm this is, in fact, the house. The mud plot that once held his half has been successfully reseeded and regrassed. The northeastern side of the structure, shorn by bulldozer, has been professionally repaired. There is no trace of damage or renovation on the home or its yard or the bordering street, at least not that Shaker can observe. It's almost as if Shaker never lived there at all.

The only new detail is on the side yard. A young man is laid horizontal on an outdoor massage table, bench-pressing a rod hung with paint pails. The pails are full of phonebooks. The kid is counting his reps aloud while some feet away the Hooster girl reclines in an old deck chair, broodily scrolling through her phone, refusing to watch him. She looks miserable, half-frittered. The kid sits up, kisses his bicep, and guzzles an orange energy drink mixed in a vodka bottle. Shaker, parked in the truck across the street, tries to salute the shirtless lothario. The kid sees him and flicks a middle finger in response.

Shaker drives off before the Hooster girl has a chance to look up.

*

The rest of the day, he dangles twenty feet off the ground via homemade harness and pulley system, burnishing the monument's haunches with fine-grit sandpaper. His arm has gone numb from so much incessant rubbing. Also, at this elevation, his nosebleeds return. The gore seems to be flooding from every artery, inlet, and nook. Twin knots of tissue are twisted from his nostrils. As they reach peak saturation, Shaker pulls them out of his face and wads them into the monument's fissures, like jelly filling in a donut.

Later, he rappels down his rope and lands on the new base, a granite slab he permanently borrowed from a Revolutionary War memorial down the road. Shaker glances around. He has nothing left to sand, so he packs up the truck and unpacks it and repacks it. A distant pinhole of sunlight continues to illuminate him despite his sincerest pleas and gripes.

Over on a distant hill of trash, a tall stranger with a scalloped haircut is watching him.

*

The microphone is hung from the chandelier, a second one slotted between stair rails, the third and fourth angled across the foyer tile, and another in the drooping begonia petals. The woman hunkers over the tape machine, her finger raised to her lips, shushing Shaker, who stands mid-foyer in a condition of near-pious confusion. She closes her eyes and bobs her head in absolute silence. She checks her watch. She holds high her arm, as if conducting a symphony's concluding note, and then she clicks off the tape machine and pries the

189

padded headphones from her ears. They are sweat-suctioned to the sides of her head.

"You're really going at this silence thing in a heavy way."

She doesn't speak, just stands there squishing the headphones together like a moist concertina. The actual concertina is wedged under a stack of rack-mounted preamps, propping them up.

"Steak tonight?" Shaker hefts the grocery sack.

"I'm fasting."

"Royce?"

"Only if you purée it."

"I can handle that."

"Wonderful."

"There's a strange man standing on the lawn," Shaker says. He points out the foyer window to the tall, mop-headed gentleman in flannel shirt and denim pants, spoked upright on the fake sod. "He's been trailing me all week."

"That's Spall," she says, barely looking.

"An old flame?"

"Of course."

"Why is he following *me*?"

"Well, it makes sense in a way." Her face retains its blanched beauty, sweet and elliptical, with all the expressiveness of a vacuum cleaner dressed in an Amish frock. "He's my Shaker."

"I thought I was your Shaker."

"That's a laugh."

"Royce?"

"Royce is my Royce. The one and only. But you Shakers are pretty much ubiquitous."

Shaker nods. "He seems a nut job."

"He'd have to be."

She shakes off the drapery of cords and equipment and presses her face so close to the pane, she practically merges with her opaque reflection. When she turns back around, she indulges him with a sympathetic pout. "Don't be sore."

He kicks a foot through the snaked cables, the sprawly space. "I'm starting to miss the banjo yodels, that's all."

"The world begins in silence, the world ends in silence. There is symmetry, a natural shape. Full circle. As a concept, it works for me. But the acoustics in here really fucking blow. I mean, seriously? This silence absolutely sucks."

"What kind of name is Spall anyway?" Shaker asks, already up the stairs and through the hall and motionless under the shower nozzle, a thousand cold noodles of rain.

16.

Spall is razing a dark footpath around the backyard, white shirt stained mustard, greasy bangs weighing in his face. The ground under his boots has cracked apart like hard cookie. Shaker occupies the greenhouse, which enables him to surveil in all directions. The woman is visible in the manor window with her microphone upraised. For days, she has been busy interrogating the cobwebs that have begun to thicken in baroque snowflake designs in all their overlit corners. She's shunning song, shunning speech. Royce has been wheeled to the dinner table to rest among the other diminished vegetation. Even he seems a bit pestered by the petty zealotries that are coopting their daily lives and annexing their house.

Shaker bends his attention back to Spall. The pacer is staying in his circuit. He pauses, realigns his feet, reverses course. Shaker is reminded of the homeless men who still mill around the monument at irregular intervals. As an awkward adolescent, Shaker never had the people skills to join the social clubs, the teams, the allegiances. He never had the *people*. Now he has his own cabal of wayward marauders, a whole tribe, plus the one straggler. The responsibility may be too much. Shaker is tracing the man's movements with the business end of an antique Winchester replica he found under a pile of anthropology textbooks in a closet upstairs. Sighting down the barrel, he feels all the blood in his body coagulating in his trigger finger. Malignant cells. Unrepentant plasmas. All the small libels of the soul.

An hour later, they try dinner. They *try* to try it. Royce will not accept the paste that the woman has mashed mortar-and-pestle style in a Stone Age crock. His facial stubble has reached whisker proportions, so Shaker leans across the table to give the man a quick trim with his butter knife, and nobody stops him. Disappointed, he rescinds the offer. Dinner decorum persists. The woman is a day and a half into a hunger strike of her own. The only fluid she is willing to ingest without force or intravenous assistance is sugar water, which Shaker didn't even realize was a legitimate beverage. Her stomach grouses so loudly throughout the meal, he says it deserves its own placemat and bib. Then he goes back to glaring at his plate of underdone sirloin as if it was hacked from his own hip. They have exhausted their supply of canned yams and canned tuna and canned spam, and yet nobody finds this a topic worthy of regard. They're trying to eat dinner, and it is only ten o'clock in the morning.

The whole house seems to be tilting a little too much into the murk.

So Shaker is not entirely surprised when he finds Spall standing aloofly in the middle of the house in rubber sandals and a sari of familiar bath towels, head stuffed in a shower cap. Twice more, Shaker catches the lanky man loafing up the stairs with several slices of bread on a plate and a bottle of ketchup. Spall is walking about in cotton socks barbarically torn at the tip, his brown, pronged toenails curling out, like starved tree roots.

"My mongrels have followed me here," Shaker announces, although the foyer is empty and his voice is not confident.

At least the lurker has an appetite in addition to fastidious table manners. Spall helps saw Royce's slab of honey-glaze chicken into edible morsels, holding the cutlery with a dainty grip, exaggerated posture. Evidently, he has been rehearsing. Two seats over, Shaker has forgone utensils altogether and licks the glaze off his plate until the surface sparkles.

He is thinking about maybe giving his Pilates another shot.

*

Although it is not his idea, Shaker fetches the stack of blankets and pest spray and binoculars from his various hidey-holes around the manor, and all four of them venture across the yard. There is a massaging quality to the evening, a radiant balm. Their motley beach party settles on the far side of the greenhouse. The woman sits with her chin resting on Royce's knees, absently stroking his emaciated doll legs as everyone looks upward, stargazing in silence. The moon looms above like an act of substantial oratory itself. At some point, the woman starts to hum, breaks off, starts again. Her melody is simple, monotonous. What first reminds Shaker of the clandestine language of religious cults and the lunatic faithful keeps devolving. Private murmur, baby babble. Royce blinks in mild ecstasy as she rubs his knee harder and harder. The woman starts to kiss his thigh, and the hum hardens in anger. Shaker touches his own throat and realizes the tetchy noise is his. All the years and miles and oceans of glue fumes he thought were lost inside him—hoovered up his sinus cavity, sealed tight—seem to be streaming out his pores in one sudden, horrific flush. His clothing is soaked through, and he can't stop wringing his vocal cords. Shaker politely excuses himself and goes to the garage. There he sits in the pressurized airlock of the SUV's backseat and screams his brainless brains out.

*

The view is difficult in the dark. Shaker senses the altitude more than he sees it as he perches atop his monument, legs swaying. Thirty-six feet of glued junk teeters underneath him like a stack of dirty dishes or an amusement park ride. He tries to stay steady, tries to focus on the spread of gray landfill below and afar when, out of the darkness, something pops him in the face. It is soft, barely solid. Then another comes whistling past his ear. A third item catches Shaker in the cheek and drops into his lap. A pinecone. Someone is chucking pinecones at him. This person's arm, Shaker realizes, is quite marvelous. Shaker reaches around the monument's rim and pries off a chunk of slag, waits for another pinecone, and hurls the slag in that direction. Then he pries another piece and hurls this, too. A fusillade commences. Pinecone and junk are shunted back and forth in lazy trajectories that Shaker has trouble tracking at this late hour. He catches a few more in the face and swallows the insult with a neutral attitude. And the tower that Shaker sits atop, rocking on its narrow crux? Even after the fusillade concludes and Shaker tiredly shimmies down to flat ground and slumps off to bed? The monument holds its height in all this new altitude and dark.

*

"Who can trust the dude?" the woman whispers. "We didn't invite him to *live* with us. He tromped in without a word or any belongings, just those hick boots and churlish demeanor, and made himself at home. What a creeper! He doesn't try to communicate. No civic etiquette. Sometimes I think he does it on purpose. Almost like a performance. I know you understand. There's a hundred different types of silence, thousands maybe, and he has *weaponized* his. That arrogant indolence. You can be sure there's some scary, insecure self-loathing underneath it all. Who knows where he goes at night? What awfulness he causes? And those toenails! His sideburns are not nearly as nice as yours. I mean, look at him! Just look at him!"

Shaker sits up and shines the flashlight. The beam catches her seated on a breakfast nook stool with her legs folded under a camouflage-patterned nighty-thingy, mud mask on her face. It is midnight at the earliest. Beside her, Spall sits on an identical stool, listening intently to her speech, nodding, nodding, still nodding.

*

He wakes on the living room couch with an unopened package of disposable paper plates balanced on his abdomen and some sort of tofu-cracker-paste concoction smeared around his mouth. Still nighttime, but all the lights are on. As far as he can remember, he dozed off elsewhere. He's not sure when he gave up sleeping in the basement. The living room is too hot for blankets, bedclothes, skin, blood, etc. From his nest on the couch, Shaker is in close proximity, although he has to peer around the packaged plates to see it fully.

The Tudor adjacent to Agog Manor is engulfed.

The orange fireball is so large and incomprehensible Shaker can't help but whistle. Someone shushes him, and Shaker realizes he is not alone in the living room. The woman is pressed to the sliding glass door, her figure small and shapeless inside a mismatched pair of Royce's animal pajamas. Shaker joins her, realizing, too, that in all this bedlam he has neglected to put on pants. Triangulating the pair is Spall, a sleep mask pushed high on his forehead, hair shag spouting out the top. The enormous flames across the yard are pointed like steeples and tails and lash around, unsynched against the roving police lights. All the spasmodic color bounces off Shaker and his dirty t-shirt, which is not quite stretchy enough to hike down over his dangling genitals. Fire engines ram the street with noise. The room throbs with secondhand heat. Shaker peeks at the spot of bare skin where the woman has rolled up her pajama leg to scratch a fresh welt. The vestige, he suspects, of some blindly hurled slag.

Shaker puts an arm around the woman, and she lets him keep it there a moment. He makes a wisecrack about holding an impromptu pot luau at the greenhouse. She smothers a halfhearted yawn. Spall swabs a fingertip around in his ear and smells the finger. On the other side of the glass, a pair of firemen—who are dousing the blaze with a torrential gush of water—exchange glances, confer with their wristwatches, then hand off their hose to another batch of firemen. The pair withdraws to a shadeless area beside their truck. They wrench off their gloves and helmets and hunt around their bunker coats. One fireman brings up a pack of cigarettes, the other furnishes a lighter. They stand in the false daylight and smoke, watching the Tudor flames bulge and leap, a still life of pitiless solitude, nonchalantly spanking the embers that stowed away on their clothes.

*

The morning light angles through the beaded curtain to incriminate Shaker alone on the kitchen floor. A tablecloth wraps his waist in a kind of antiquarian kilt, and his face has been mysteriously washed clean. He looks through the doorway to the den. Royce remains a stoic boulder sculpted into his wheelchair. The invalid's eyes are open, his vision unwavering. The TV is blank glass. Somewhere below them in the basement, the woman flits around with an omni-directional mic and thirty feet of kinked cable, recording every strain and stress of the manor's foundation, the stillness, the absence, the new frontier.

Spall is outside at the brown seam of the backyard where fake grass turns to cinder. He's holding a washcloth in one hand and a book of matches in the other, bobbling both.

Ordinarily, Shaker would board up the windows and nail shut the doors, fill the chimney flue with saltwater taffy and broken glass, every entrance and orifice occluded, closed. He's already composing the punch list in his head. Then he remembers all his construction materials were absorbed into the monument long ago.

*

The Tullys have their usual consortium of rakes and tweezers and sieves loaded in the truck, and they don't grab any of them, either. Rather than panning for remainders, the Brothers are kicking a clean avenue through the Tudor rubble with Shaker drafting in their wake. They ignore the smoldered heap of patio accoutrement, a heavily dimpled dartboard, several ceramic busts of Beethoven and J. Robert Oppenheimer, a tetherball glued with razorblades that the blowfish junkies must have exploited in some hallucinatory parlor game.

Spall loiters on his small area, watching them blankly.

"The thing is," Shaker tells him, "we're gonna need you to go ahead and vacate the, uh, the whole, you know...this whole place. Think of it as a Spall-free zone. My associates are ready to assist in any way."

The Tullys exchange impatient glares. Shaker finds a blackened box of dog biscuits underfoot and pops a treat into Spall's mouth. In an act of solidarity, Shaker pops another into his own. Tastes like fireplace. Both men continue chewing, nodding and chewing, until Spall plods off the property, his head slung, like a defeated second-stringer snipped from the JV roster.

"Seems a sensible enough chap," Shaker says, squinting at the man's retreat. "You think that worked?"

The Brothers are already scooping, sieving, tweezing.

"I think that worked," Shaker says.

*

When the woman wanders out back to demand Shaker return to the kitchen and finish apportioning the smoked rump of ham nobody much wants to eat for their fourth dinner of the day, she has to clear the greenhouse to find him. Shaker is still standing in the empty rubble. The Tullys are gone, Spall is gone. At his feet, a medium-height pile of mud and clay he has begun to shape into a sullen sandcastle, already crumbling.

"Just trying to add a few extra turrets," he mumbles.

The woman is not wearing her usual panda makeup. She's dressed drab, unremarkable. At the same time, some puritanical string or cable has come loose inside Shaker, made him reckless and tipsy, and he presses against her. She tolerates the kiss for a few tepid seconds, long enough for Shaker to realize that special cable inside him is not slack at all, it is stiffening, intensely carnal, so urgent he may begin to lose oxygen along with common sense and geographic bearings. The woman steps back. The kiss is vanished, a relic. Only a sad vacancy remains.

"Explain it to me," Shaker says. "One of your men can't rouse himself out of his pj's, let alone wheelchair.

199

The other is a clueless arsonist who needs a stepladder to boost his IQ."

"And then there's Spall," she says with a sarcastic twinkle. It fizzles immediately.

"I'm not going to mention the guys in the trucks. Your, uh, customers."

"All very nice, lonely blokes who have the distinct advantage of not being you."

"Would you like to see me eat dirt?" Shaker asks.

"Much worse."

"My hair, my scalp."

"I used to have a terrible fear about hair. How it just keeps growing and growing and growing."

"The dead need barbers, too," Shaker says knowingly.

"In a perfect world, I could just click my heels together and send you streaking down the road with all your skin on fire, a hardboiled egg clenched between your butt cheeks."

"So I get to keep my scalp."

"I'm pregnant," she says.

Shaker is casting about, prodding his pockets, distracted. "Must be some matches here, somewhere."

She grabs his arm, harder than he expected. "It's not your zygote."

"Maybe it is."

"It's Royce's."

"How would that work?" Shaker asks. "Did you use a turkey baster? Hook a car battery up to his prostate? Maybe one day I'd *like* a zygote."

His pocket contents: gum wrapper, gas receipt, eleven different species of lint. Shaker sifts the collection with a fingernail and claps it all from his hands.

"It may not even be real," she says. "Sometimes my uterus gets confused. It swells up, makes me sick, then sheds itself. The dream is purged. I'm sure I'm not the only one. Biology is an irrational thing. Almost like love, you know? Love is just a lie your body believes."

Shaker isn't sure what his face is doing at the moment, but whatever the thing, it makes him shut his eyes. In the dim theater of his head, he can almost imagine the confused uterus, tyrannical and overpink, and all the heavenly gravities and earthly suctions that badger and bribe and ultimately bankrupt the poor organ. Just saying the word *zygote* has candied his brain.

Still shut-eyed, sunk in some kind of emotional gulch, he lifts up his shirt.

"This scar that looks like a triple nipple?" he says. "You gotta squint hard to see it. One night, I was skulking around the house, doing my old sleepwalking routine, and she thought I was an intruder. At least that's what the police report said. I don't remember. When she shot me, apparently I started singing. Really, really loud, bad singing. She told the cops she would have shot me a second time, just to shut me up, but the gun jammed. The gun was loaded with blanks I learned, but those things leave a nifty scar when fired at close range. Some nights, if I'm sitting perfectly still, I can almost hear the wind blowing straight through me like a harmonica. And I really hate the sound of harmonica."

A hand clamps his jiggling knee. Shaker opens his eyes.

He's only mildly surprised to find he is flat on the ground. The woman has disappeared inside the manor. The hand on his knee is his hand. He has no idea how much time has passed, if time passes at all, if he can pass with it. Somewhere to the west and east of Shaker, great pieces of landmass are flaking apart and drifting off into a weepy Technicolor sunset that makes his retinas ache.

Empires are falling extinct, animal kingdoms closing up shop. The evicted dead are trundling through a frumpy and overpopulated afterlife, still dressed in their funeral best. At some point, Shaker knows he, too, will rise. He'll loaf and shirk and scramble, repeating the same pitiable charade until it stops seeming like a charade. But for now, he can only lay here, raddled and prone, craning his neck like an idiot sunflower trying to bend a little bit nearer the light.

17.

The dome is a skeleton of studs and struts and a plywood base, rainbow hued, large and finished. It holds the children's attention like no slouching tower of badly cobbled trash ever could. The children have formed an outer ring that shrinks around the dome until the two geometries touch. There are rebukes from their teacher, but Darb waves the woman away. Crouching at kid level, he remarks, "Damn thing is meant to be touched. Really feel it, guppies." He hoists a girl, sandy blond and squirmy, draping her over a crossbar. Soon the entire class is bustling up the naked scaffold, forty feet in height, like a playground jungle gym. Inside the dome, two boys are shadowing their classmates' movements and poking them with sticks, grabbing at bare feet, shoes lost. A photographer pinned with press credentials is worming around the grass, shooting from a variety of perspectives, as chaperoning parents take pictures of the cameraman with their children artfully arranged in the background. The whole scene makes Shaker want to shove a clotheswire up his own insides and snake it around until all the plaque has been scraped loose. Make a kebab of the knotted animal. Straighten things right out.

But he's still feeling some residual guilt for the health code complaint that he filed last week—paperwork so far ignored by local officials—so he pays to enter the grounds, plunking his two dollars in nickels and pennies into a coffee canister speared on a pillar. The pillar is a rickety pike, a monument in miniature. Shaker gives it a little sneer and steps through the ramshackle gate that leads to more metal fence. The barbed border stretches around several acres of land. The dead oaks have been felled. The ground is carpeted in artificial turf. In a far corner rests a stockpile of donated cat food tins, repair supplies, welding equipment, a lemonade and souvenir stand. A portable radio broadcasts theme park melodies. Shaker waits as Darb helps the last child down from the dome, shakes hands with the teacher and chaperones and the media contingent, and stands in the road waving farewell to the rusted school bus retreating into the distance. Darb turns to Shaker and cranks his head in a rotary motion, left and right and left, some demure cartilage cracking in his neck.

"This shit exhausts me, man. I'm just trying to stay busy, you know? Keep following the bouncing ball, not get distracted. But goddamn." Darb finishes cracking himself and slaps at the collection canister. It twirls round on its lone nail hinge, a wobbly orbit. "Fucking thing is a disaster."

"The dome draws a crowd."

"Dookie has its flies, too."

"Are those refrigerator magnets?" Shaker eyeing the souvenir stand.

"I got another classroom arriving in five minutes."

"I finally heard back from the planning department. I asked for a few zoning variances, height variances. They replied with a cease-and-desist letter. I guess the trash hill is an old, historic Indian territory. I called their bluff. Told them I'm one-sixteenth Navajo. Haven't heard back yet."

But Darb is still gazing at his own dome. "The longer it stands, the more I despise it."

"Maybe if I rent—"

"Dynamite," Darb says.

"Pardon?"

"You can talk to your Tully friends for me. They are connected. Demolition shit, drug shit, *shit* shit. That's how I got the port-a-potties installed out here. But they ain't returning my calls about the explosives. I do love those dudes. Can you tell 'em apart? One has a lisp impediment. Subtle, but it's there. I think that one's Derrick. Other one is Bo. The muscle."

"They're both muscle."

"Muscle isn't everything," Darb shrugs, spitting some heavy lung curd in the dirt. "I'm talking about blowing this bastard up with TNT."

Shaker nods steadily. "Is this a drug thing or a schizo thing?"

Darb immediately stiffens. When he speaks, it's with an odd quiver in his lip.

"That's unkind, cousin. Where's the sweet, old Shaker who was once my best pal and visited my woman and tried to play daddy with my boy while I was off on business? Really dug himself in. Probably happened right about here."

Darb stomps the ground a few times, then clasps his arms behind his back, holding himself at parade rest. "I'm just gonna let you wonder what else I know and what I think I know."

"Okay-o," Shaker says slowly.

"No." His cousin does not blink. "Maybe it ain't o-fucking-kay-o."

Darb spreads his legs into a wide stance and mimes a few jujitsu moves. "Behold the avenging spirit!"

A high kick nearly catches Shaker in the throat.

"Stop fucking around," Shaker says.

"Avenging spirit knows kung fu and tai chi and eleven kinds of karate. Got the memory of an elephant. He pays his taxes on time."

Shaker is unable to move more than a foot, half a foot, really, angling into the road where his cousin now looks, a vague glaze in Darb's eyes. Shaker wants to understand the glaze. Although that would require he remain glaze-free himself.

"You set for groceries?" he asks instead.

His cousin sighs and unfolds himself from his martial stance. "Maybe when all this craziness is over, we drag what's left of us to the Beagle. Grab some beers, me and you."

"I thought you went cold turkey."

"That's right," Darb replies. "I did, didn't I?"

He collects the two dollars in corroded change from the pay box, jingling it in a fist. Shaker pinches his lips and watches silently as Darb flings the coins into the road.

*

In open daylight, on the hills of trash, Shaker and his monument cast identical shadows, both slanting like uncertain sundials against the horizon. Shaker feels paltry, detained. His socks, at present, are dry. The wide scope of the rubbish field parallels the sky in color and grain, a suspicious optical illusion that Shaker does not trust. All these interlocking repetitions. The planet continues its nonstop eastward creep, machinery clanging. The high breezes that have whooshed in and trampled this derelict fleck of Ohio are still looping around the earth. Shaker wonders if he is degrading with each cycle, or does the repetition ratify him instead, make him more and more like himself? Who would that be, exactly? And is there any real difference between all the potential versions of him unloosed into the ether, barbecue sauce on their chins, a tired glitch in their expressions? He knocks loose a rock and plays an abbreviated round of soccer, flubs his penalty kick, and that's when he sees them coming. His homeless tribe. They sway down the cratered hill in tight automaton ranks, holding fast to the land. Shaker half-expects to hear them humming sacred fugues and dissonant hymns, but the men remain silent. So Shaker licks his cracked lips and whistles for them. He really throws himself into the act, running alongside the ragged caravan, screeching, flapping his arms. Their gray faces are downturned, shrunken in their hoods. They ignore the chirpy lunatic striding beside them in some kind of trash-field steeplechase. Shaker hurries to the front of the procession, gets a short lead, and successfully forms a one-man blockade. The group comes to a lethargic stop. Shaker is startled by the cooperation; he hadn't expected that part. He shifts foot to foot, saliva hanging off his squished lips, chagrined.

"Just a simple hello," Shaker says. "Even a head nod, a handshake. Any reaction at all."

The leader is shortish and glum-faced under a harsh thicket of beard. A pair of scrumbled, undiscerning eyes stare back at Shaker. Shaker takes hold of the man's chin and softly squeezes the gray cheeks, popping the man's mouth open. That cavity is gray, too, desiccated. The man lacks a tongue. Shaker releases him and grabs the next one and squeezes. Then he grabs another and another and another. All of them tongueless.

"You cut them out," Shaker says. "Why did you cut them out?"

Shaker's shame is too much, even for him. He lets go of the last man and touches his own mouth. That pointless, frowning mass. Shaker steps aside and aims a finger at the monument.

"It's all yours now," he says. "I just can't stick my landings anywhere."

But the homeless men only stare at him blankly and turn and shuffle back up the trash slope, over the hill, gone into that tiny crag of horizon where land and sky cleave together and apart.

*

Shaker stirs until nightfall. He has showered all the hot water out of the manor, toweled his skin furiously, and removed his mutton-chop sideburns by burning off each individual hair with a lit match. He tries not to look at the foot. Intermittent rain batters the rooftop and windows with the plinking cadence of scattershot artillery. Shaker limps around the upstairs, nosing his whole face into the woman's warm roll of laundry. Next comes a quick trip to the basement to wrangle up some ancient board games for Royce. He changes the sock every ten to fifteen minutes. One hour and a half-dozen argyles later, Shaker is presenting a snarl of jump ropes to the invalid man, a deck of tarot cards, three roller-skate wheels, and a nonfunctioning dehumidifier. Royce watches the exchange with a box of Chinese takeout wedged in his lap. The chopsticks are taped to his fingers. Several rooms away, the woman is retching into the echo chamber of a porcelain toilet bowl. A sound so tawny, so hollow.

"Morning sickness," Shaker says. "At eleven o'clock at night."

He spears a lump of noodle strands and dangles them into Royce's mouth. Then he takes Royce's jaw and jiggers it open and closed. Royce emits a succinct gurgle of happiness. It's the most emotion the man has exhibited all year.

"Sounds like she's really going for it in there," Shaker says. "The vomit-triumvirate."

Holding the box to his own face like a feed sack, Shaker slurps a few entwined noodles and chews them with scholarly consideration. "Sometimes people say the name Shaker to me, and my only thought is furniture. Really feebleminded furniture."

He can feel Royce gazing up into the hairy murk of his nostrils.

"You may be the better man," Shaker whispers at him, "but both of us are highly flammable."

Shaker scans the hall again to make sure the woman is still in the bathroom. He lifts his leg, drops it across the table, and peels off the bloody sock. Royce doesn't react, but Shaker gags at the sight of his foot, swollen and gory, an unpleasant plum color.

He struggles to resheath it with a clean sock.

"When I came home this afternoon, I found a flaming pile on our doorstep. I tried to stomp it out." Shaker reaches into the kitchen trash and pulls out the charred mass of numerous blowfish glued together, spikes jutting, bent, bloody. He slams the ball back into the bin. "Any guesses?"

The bathroom echoes are reverberating down the hall. Shaker takes up the chopsticks and begins to frantically shovel more noodles into Royce's mouth, a riotous swarm in at least one of their brains.

*

The woman is dozing on a collapsible deck chair among all the overgrown nature inside their shimmering, imperial greenhouse. In addition to hunger striking, she has undertaken an ambitious vow of silence. Several of them.

The plant life around her is raw and thriving. Royce is also asleep, his wheelchair leveraged against the bay window on the second-floor landing. He is immersed in his favorite lumberjack flannel, a beret tilted rakishly on that beautiful, gray head. The Winchester replica is propped in his hands. The gentleman looks like he is settling in for the long siege.

The house is quiet. The quiet is cacophonous.

Shaker clambers into the truck and drives, but he cannot find any indication of Spall. The mop-haired arsonist has either receded too far into the distance or is lurking just outside Shaker's peripheral vision. Shaker finds himself gliding along the same circular path that delineates the outermost edge of town. It's late, it's dark. Darb is not at the dome, but the dome is still standing. Shaker has armed himself with a flashlight and roadmap, and he marches the field's barb-knotted border, its shallow depressions, its ambiguous seepages, not entirely sure who or what he's pursuing at this point. A mordant image soon comes to mind. He sees his cousin hitchhiking to Tuscaloosa with a belt of trophy scalps, cat bone necklace, a Tupperware full of ash under his arm. Darb has always been so fussy about his totems. His clinging nature betrayed the soft naïveté under all that stubborn delirium. Shaker suspects his own clinging, by contrast, has always lacked that honor, lacked that wanton love.

Shaker takes in the landscape, wide-spanning, here to there, the ultimate purview. He's lightheaded from so much squinting in the dark, and it does something extraordinary to his vision. The periphery looks radioactively aglow at this hour. Overhead are runaway satellites and planetoids and free-floating exobiological stations, a million stray tons of space junk burning up on reentry. Maybe one or two astronauts marooned in the soup. There is a faint rim of scarlet that announces the tree line. The sky looks rouged. Shaker groggily climbs down the bric-a-brac hemisphere of his cousin's dome as if descending the wired-together bones of a museum brontosaur, the sky ablaze with rock dust and dying light.

For almost an hour, he drives the town. He even visits the landfill, but there is only the tall stack of his tower. His tribe is gone. The hazmat is packed up. Back inside the truck, Shaker fixes the lank monument in his rearview mirror and decides to keep it there, always behind him, a solitary grave marker with some glue-poisoned fool barnacled to its flank. That guy can stay there, too.

On the way back to Agog Manor, he stops at the Tully compound to return the hazmat. He's even stuffed it in its original gift box. Their house is dark except the living room. Shaker smutches his face against the windowpane and can see some furniture and various personal effects in outline, the aquarium's phosphorescent gleam. Rather than slam into the door and re-break his collarbone, Shaker takes the prudent action and knocks. The door swings wide. He shrugs off the sense of déjà vu, scuffs the mud from his steel-toed shitkickers, and moseys inside.

The house is odorless, more sedate and extraterrestrial than Shaker remembers. There are respiratory sounds in the room that may or may not belong to him. The fish tank burbles. The rug is bunched underfoot. Shaker fumbles about blindly, and when he turns on a lamp he finds both Tullys splayed on the floor as if making snow angels, neat lilac bullet wounds in the middle of their foreheads. Blood is spattered in identical floral designs where the rug has been scrunched up. There is brain goop limned between the naked floorboards. Each red canal looks like a vibrant artery, still pulsing, inching along the hardwood, alive.

The sight is too much. Shaker's stomach surges and he's knocked forward by the need to vomit. Yet he can't quit staring at the dumbfounded visages the Tullys have attained in death. They look positively stupefied. Like children gone to some miserable circus—long lines, lame animals, stale cotton candy—only to be surprised they had a much better time than expected.

The bile that Shaker spits up misses the carpet completely. He has no tissue to wipe his mouth so he uses his hand, trembling, like meat on a stick. A rustling draws his attention. Someone is resting in the BarcaLounger with a pistol balanced on his kneecap. Where the man normally has a head is only black rubber, dark lens. The empty gaze of Mort's gasmask. It fits him rather well.

"Did you know the word *aloha*," says Darb's muffled voice, "means hello and goodbye in Hawaiian?"

"You executed them," Shaker mumbles, his own gray matter pancaked against the wall of his skull. Sort of centrifugally flung there. "They're dead."

"Nope," Darb says. "They're saying *aloha*."

Darb pushes the mask up so the mouthpiece rests on his forehead like a third eye, his cheeks smothered red. He has been crying again.

"Death ain't such a bad trip," Darb sniffles. He extends his forearms with the pink scars that crosscut each wrist. The scars appear to be smiling. "I always loved being a little sad as a kid. A little sadness gives you that righteous burn. That's the thing that keeps you intact. Bonds you with other folk. We're all just simpatico amigos being a little sad in the world together, singing *aloha* in chorus. In jail, the sad got bigger each day. I used the zipper on my pants, but I slashed the wrong veins. Took them fifteen minutes to find me, and in that time I swum the River Styx and come back. Know what it feels like? Parasailing. Death feels like parasailing with your intestine strings hanging way the fuck out."

Darb rises and belts the pistol and prods each Tully with his foot.

"Just ask them," he says.

"Uh, Darb?"

"All these fucking wars in Ye Old Arabia. Pisses me off. Why can't people be goddamn nicer to each other? We gotta be strivers, you know? That's why the blowfish thing, the puffer fish thing. I had dealings, I admit. I took some trips. That's interstate traffic, cousin. An entire book of federal statute they can throw at you. And, god, is it a morose scene in Pennsyl-tucky. Whole operations are seeded there, distribution centers, underground cells. A grand network. You know the trick with fixing pimples? You had a rough face as a teen, so you can attest. You gotta squish them on the first try or else they come back in a havoc."

He gives the Tullys a harder kick.

"I'm just trying to be a good dude in my own amazing way," he says.

"They were pals of mine."

"Mine too," Darb says. "But only after I squished them."

Shaker realizes his own foot is blocking the sanguine ravine of Tully blood. He picks it up and sets it down in exactly the same spot. "They were just black marketeers selling bootlegged crap and trading favors for favors."

"Let's clean up this mess," says Darb.

"You blew up your—"

"Clean with me," says Darb, "or it'll be four bodies that need burying."

He makes a pistol of his fingers and holds it to the rubber item that crowns his head. Shaker has lost mobility, voltage. He watches, tame and vapid, as his cousin reaches down and plucks the truck keys from a Tully pocket.

"You drag, I'll drive," Darb says. "Shovels are already in the truck."

Shaker is too numb to say no. He understands that part. Really, he does. What mystifies him more than anything else, though, is the noise his mouth makes when it opens wide and announces in a mild tone: "I know the perfect spot."

*

Springtime has relaxed the rubbish. Shaker slices loosely with his shovel, never needing to saw or heave or stab or whack. His arms are steered by muscle memory, repetition, as easy as tunneling through warm marmalade. Oddly, it's a kind of joy. Then Shaker recognizes the joy, and his innards clamp up. He leans harder into the work, swinging enough shoulder and hip to knock a hole through the continental shelf, wherever that is. It's only a hole, he thinks. Only a hole. The Tully corpses are swaddled in their rug, taped shut. Darb is whamming about with a pickax he found on the premises. Once the hole is made, he uses the pickax to undo the tape. Briskly and without much ceremony, he unrolls the Tullys into their shallow grave. Then he rolls the carpet up and drags it back to the truck.

"It's a nice rug," he shrugs as Shaker gawks from the ledge of their morbid crater. "That wood floor in the living room would just depress me, and I don't think I can get all the ectoplasm wiped away. Probably stained in there. What luck they didn't bleed any on this beauty."

"You're taking their house."

"Waste not," he sighs.

"I think I'm gonna be sick again."

"You know where the hole is."

But it's only a dry retch. Shaker looks up, looks around. "Somewhere out here is the Minnesotan. You remember him?"

"I do not."

"He's a goddamn ghost," Shaker says.

"Well, now he won't be so alone, yeah?"

"We should say something for them."

Darb spins around a few times, searching for an audience, a verification of some type. "We're burying them, ain't we? You need more poetry than that?"

"Yes," Shaker says.

"Floor is yours, senator."

Shaker peers into the dim, crumbled cavity, waiting for something inside him to well up—grief, disgrace, any penitent slobber—but the dryness still clings his throat. He kicks in a few rocks, takes out his wallet, and tosses it in the hole.

"Genius!" Darb bellows. "Leave some evidence! You wanna throw in a pair of your white undies with your name scribbled on the waistband, too?"

"They'll ID me by my dental work."

"Huh?"

"I'm saying if you want me in a different hole, make sure you knock out my teeth."

Darb's face undergoes an incredible cycle of contortions, broad, tight, elastic, before returning to its original confusion.

"You upset me with that kind of talk," Darb says. "I ain't stone-hearted, and I ain't a killer. The redeemer does the dirty work. All of us are just antennas for the divine."

"Shaker," he adds. "Hey, Shakes? You want a hand pushing in all that dirt?"

But Shaker is too busy ramming the mound of ash and churned stuff back to its source. Darb sighs again and takes up the second shovel, scooping furiously at the trash, the sinews in his neck large and red with throb. He's racing Shaker, but Shaker is oblivious, shoveling steadily, the dirt lobbed in orderly arcs. When the hole is no more and the coarse ground is patched together to match the rest of the topography, the men throw their shovels into the pickup. And Shaker, shivering in his sweat, stomach sick, limbs filthy: He points to his monument, moonlit and pale in the distance.

"Help me push it over," he says.

"You serious?"

"It'll only take a minute."

Darb chews the interior of his cheek so strenuously his whole face furrows. The distortion signals a sour and waggling thought.

"Let it stand," Darb says. "The boy probably would've liked it, in his own slow way. He liked pointless things."

Shaker can see the sutures in his cousin's face splitting, the whole red rock breaking apart.

"That secret committee of folks that fucked with your furniture and plumbing and plowed down your house? Man, I'm on that committee," Darb says. "Problem is, there's so many members it takes forever to make a decision about anything. We're talking years and years of gabbing and quorums and bureaucracy shit. The whole town, pretty much. Tullys introduced me to them, and they introduced me to the shadiness across the border. Pennsyl-tucky mafia. Ain't no joke. I was trying to promote the blowfish, you know? Build the brand and all? Had to really spin it hard 'cause that shit sounds sorta bonkers and too much of it makes you chew your tongue off at the root. Maybe I sorta oversold the operation. Mafia bastards must have torched my fucking house before the ink on the contract was even dry. That's my guess. The whole thing was probably a sham, a setup. They were just weeding out the competition. So I did some weeding of my own. Had to start somewhere." Darb nodding at the dirt. "Still not sure how bad I'm supposed to feel about all this. But I really did try to relish it."

His mouth is open, his nose and eyes wet.

"Maybe it's true," he adds, "I was not the most stringent of daddies."

Darb shakes the gasmask off his forehead and cradles it carefully in the crook of his elbow, like an infant or booby-trapped parcel, on his walk back to the truck.

*

Shaker's one solemn act with a firearm came years ago, when he purchased a pistol to assassinate a family of squirrels that had invaded the attic of the farmhouse he and his singer-girlfriend were renting in the woodlands, near a scenic Superfund site. The constant scamperings and scratchings resonated throughout the house all night, every night. Traps, poisoned acorns, tainted cheese. Every ploy failed to incapacitate the vermin. So Shaker bought a pistol his cousin had recommended a little too loudly, a long-snouted, silver-plated thing, which he needed both hands to hold and some assistance to aim. Shaker blasted so many divots and clefts in the attic roof the rain flooded through, collapsing the insulation into the wood, and the wood into the plaster, all those layers sandwiched and buckling. Soon the entire house was infested with rain rot. Conditions grew uninhabitable for squirrel and human alike. Shaker and his girlfriend spontaneously eloped after she used the same gun to shoot him at point-blank range one night, and for six months they moved among a series of rental trailers and motel rooms until she realized her true error and moved on without him. Shaker pawned the gun for a better brand of radio. The squirrels were replaced by roaming dogs that have likewise fled to some faraway locale. But Shaker remains, grouchily leaned in the passenger seat while Darb drives in silence, the roadside streaking in drips and squiggles.

"I'm fine with not speaking," Darb says. "Silence doesn't rankle me like it does some."

"Then shut up."

"Make me, mountebank."

"Fancy talk."

"Got it from a book. I'm a reader, you know."

"What a brain loaf," Shaker says as the pickup bounces a pothole. Darb's revolver rests on the dashboard. The turbulence slides it a little closer to Shaker's side.

Darb is staring with enormous focus on the road. "That's the one thing that baffles me with this whole cryogenic freeze business. Why do the scientists save only your head? That's the most useless part of the pig."

"Depends on the pig," Shaker says, glimpsing his own reflection in the windshield, his doltish lips, lumpy eyelids, flattened face. The relief of the survivor and the stupidly living everywhere upon him. It is a look of minor existence, and it's not a look he savors.

"You're a killer," Shaker mutters at the reflection. "It's not enough to bear the dark. You have to bear the pallor, the sunlight."

"Say what?" Darb asks.

"Sunlight," Shaker says.

"You ain't looking so hot."

"I feel fine, absolutely fine. I need to go on some kind of epic vision quest, and you need more time in prison."

"Whoa now—"

"Here," Shaker says. "Let me help."

Shaker snatches the pistol from the dashboard and cracks it open. Four bullets remain. He folds it shut, brandishing the weapon just out of his cousin's reach.

"Watch where you point that hair dryer," Darb says.

"Nervous?"

"You won't shoot me."

"No," Shaker says. "I won't."

And he presses the barrel into his own thigh, the swell of meat there, the muscle and knot, and he fires a round pure as sunshine itself. The pain squeezes through his flesh and femur and maybe the floorboards, too. For a brief moment, Shaker thinks he can hear the bullet rebound off the asphalt with a melodious ping. The truck cab fills with thunder and smoke.

"My gawd!" Darb howls as the pickup swerves. Blood has sprayed everywhere. Everything's ringing. Shaker emits the most candid babble, but Darb's the one who shouts, "Think you blew off the muffler, son!"

"Should we go back for it?" Shaker asks, woozy and shutting his eyes against the pain. The pain is all he is.

"That was balls, man! Balls!"

Darb regains his breath in increments. He has stopped pounding the steering wheel, and he's swiveling his head with less frequency.

"Leg looks foul," he says. "You know any doctors who stitch but don't snitch?"

Shaker can only grumble. The roadside is still streaking, but he's not coherent enough to absorb it.

Darb cracks his neck, tense against the wheel, the rearview mirror filling with his jaw. "Emergency room?" he asks.

Shaker's whole body is on fire, several variations, whites and reds and golds and neons, each one holier than the last.

"Parasailing," he replies.

*

The emergency room is more hallway than room, with three plastic chairs in buoyant preschool shades, a grimy communal water cooler, a nurse's station overlit with fluorescence. There are no magazines or TV. No mangled men or mauled women with handkerchief slings or homemade splints or children moaning with ruptured organs. No insurance scammers or unsuccessful suicides. The corridor is empty and the desk is unstaffed. Shaker isn't nodding in and out of consciousness so much as noodling around it. He can sense Darb, grumped and restless, in the chair beside him. Darb crosses his legs. His foot wags. Shaker registers the fabric-chafing noises, but Darb's movement and the chafe noises remain disconnected. The reason exceeds Shaker's purview. Most things do. Shaker keeps his head against the wall and tries not to regard the new wound glaring up at him like an evil, abscessed eye.

Darb gives him an elbow nudge. The woman in white, suddenly appeared at the desk, is staring at Shaker with intense boredom. Shaker clears the saliva and panic from his throat, feeling for the correct octave. Unable to string together a cohesive sentence, he simply points at his cousin and croaks, "Him did it."

"Sir?"

"Shot me. The thighbone. Ring the fuzz."

The nurse shifts her boredom to Darb, no longer tap dancing in his chair. He's peering into the dark triangle of his crossed legs, the riven sole of his disintegrating loafer, Mort's gasmask on his knee. Instead of addressing the nurse or Shaker, he consults his clenched fist. The gasmask watches him, impassive, alert.

"Kinda looks like my handiwork, sure," Darb says, flexing the fist into articulation. All it needs is a sock puppet. As the woman dials the authorities, Darb pushes a thumb up into his mouth to straighten his dentures. Finally, he looks at his cousin, too furious to speak. His dentures give one last clack. The sound is so firm, so conclusive, that Shaker fills with a mysterious relief. Maybe this is the only mercy left. Here and gone before it can be touched or autopsied or memorialized or even acknowledged at all.

Shaker sits up and says, "Probably a few more minutes before the cops get here."

"Sure," Darb replies with a bogus yawn.

Shaker moves his eyes towards the door. "Greyhound waits for no man," he adds.

Darb nods indifferently. Shaker throws another obvious glance at the doorway. Darb meets his gaze and nods again, then again and again in gradual acceleration. Shaker tries to smile, but the most he can do is wince with his posterior teeth. But Darb understands. He gives his dentures one more clack, wipes the hand on his jeans, reaches over, and sticks an index finger into the freshly steaming hole in Shaker's leg.

"Goddamn!" Shaker shouts, writhing, frantic.

The nurse looks up from her clipboard, her boredom declining into low-wattage abhorrence. Shaker cannot see much room anymore. He has the leg-on-fire pulled up to his chest. And Darb. Darb extends the blood-slick finger and the steady hand to which it is attached, examining it like a messy dipstick.

"Just making sure the nerves are all there," he says.

And Shaker, euphoric with pain, promptly passes out.

18.

Shaker is hobbling around Agog Manor on his
crutch, numbly colliding the furniture, smashed
sheetrock and dead appliances still strewn in the halls.
The painkillers have wrapped him in an angelic gauze.
Somewhere under the real dressing on his leg, the
thread and pinwork are not exactly done neat. Shaker
couldn't be happier. The woman watches his slapstick
from a middle distance, a hand on her pelvis, smiling
her vague smile at Shaker. She prepares his tomato-
and-barbiturate soup each morning and twice a day
ministers his bandages while Shaker sags in a mail-
order hammock salvaged from the basement and
suspended from pegs and hooks in the den ceiling. On
occasion, she even sings for him. She stands beside the
hammock in a girly one-piece romper that is striped
red-white-blue, hair pulled off her face by rubber band,
although several rogue curlicues disturb her pasty
forehead like misplaced punctuation marks. Shyly, she
sings a capella, gazing unbroken at him and only him.
It's a solitary performance. Her voice is tarnished and
reedy, not musical at all. But it has a scrappy charisma,
an integrity. The lyrics are a mash note of TV ads,
political stump speeches, encyclopedia entries, radio
rants, childish gibberish; a recycled misappropriation
that implicates, yet exalts, mass culture's endless loop.

The Whirling Universal Repeat. Shaker is in rabid love with every purloined word. He rises on his crutch and leans intently forward. He's ready to crank open his silly maw and finally croon along.

And then, once again, the woman is gone. No goodbye sticky note, no great pageantry or grudge sex or farewell kiss. Just gone. Royce has disappeared as well, although for reasons Shaker cannot explain their SUV is still parked in the garage. Shaker finds Royce's whole wardrobe steamed clean and regally folded in the closet upstairs, so he borrows a few favorites. Soon he's parading around the manor in every stripe and stitch the stroked man owned. Some nights, he takes his sleep without mattress or blanket, sprawled on the floor in twill and corduroy and khaki, like a well-dressed tramp. He feels like he's working on a new purview altogether. He sleeps unsoundly but wakes, strangely, with strong enthusiasms. He just isn't sure for what.

This is how they find him, flat on the sun-warmed foyer tile, hazed from a dream he can't quite reconvene. Shaker opens his eyes and discovers the older woman and older man. They are tanned and dressed in tropical pastels, astride several intimidating trunks of plaid-print luggage, hovering over Shaker's half-woken face.

"Gerald," the woman says. "This homeless man is drooling all over your corduroys. My god, I think he tried to remodel our kitchen. So much savage damage!"

Shaker awards the elderly couple an amiable look, a trustworthy look. The look of a man who contains sturdy moral textiles, astute psychological tackle, with no hint of the charlatan about him at all. When he opens his mouth to speak, though, he finds his voice has vanished.

Shaker is unable to utter a single, lucid, lifesaving word.

Acknowledgments

Great thanks and fierce gratitude are due:
Giancarlo DiTrapano.

Sam Lipsyte.

Dana Spiotta, Arthur Flowers, George Saunders, Christopher Kennedy, Christine Schutt, Gary Lutz, and all at the Syracuse University Creative Writing Program, particularly my fearless cohort—Rachel Abelson, Mildred Barya, Chanelle Benz, Martin De Leon, Rebecca Fishow.

Gene Kwak, and Ryan Ridge and Ashley Farmer for excerpting early portions of this novel via *NOÖ Journal* and *Juked*, respectively.

Jacob White and JT Tompkins for first reads.

Steve Gattine for the final gander.

Joe Kepic, Brendan Kuntz, Tom Yagielski, Kevin Dossinger, Haley Dossinger, Chris Romeis, Pat Lonergan, Travis Forte, and José Beduya for the soundtrack and the tinnitus.

Jason Nutt and Randolph Wright for early and generous and possibly misplaced encouragement.

My parents—Charles and Deborah Nutt—for their affectionate bewilderment and unstinting support.

And Gina for, well, everything.

David Nutt was born in 1977. He is a former newspaper reporter and copy editor, speechwriter, substitute teacher, executive assistant, administrative assistant, electrician's assistant, office gopher, dishwasher, grocery stocker, part-time burger flipper, begrudging paperboy, and sometime musician. His fiction has appeared in *The American Reader*, *Electric Literature's Okey-Panky*, *Green Mountains Review*, *Hobart*, *Juked*, *New York Tyrant*, *NOÖ Journal*, *Open City*, and *Washington Square Review*. He attended the MFA Program in Creative Writing at Syracuse University, where he met his wife, the poet Gina Keicher. They live in Ithaca, New York, with their dog and two cats.